WE THREE

WE THREE

A Novella By
JEWELLE GOMEZ

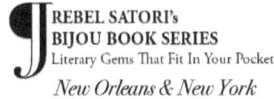

REBEL SATORI's
BIJOU BOOK SERIES
Literary Gems That Fit In Your Pocket
New Orleans & New York

Published in the United States of America by
Rebel Satori Press
www.rebelsatoripress.com

Paperback ISBN: 978-1-60864-332-5

For Joanna Russ
and Octavia E. Butler
who showed me a way
when there
was no way

I. Lynx and Strand

SESSION #77

#Like the chips of colored crystal in a kaleidoscope the twin reflections of her back moved closer together in the corner of the restaurant window as she walked through the door. The images converged in the mirrored panes of glass and vanished inside each other. Across the street a muted shadow stepped from a doorway and followed. Strand's heart thudded, she gulped for breath.

"Whoa!" Nelson said in his soft voice, easing Strand out of her anxious dream. The shadow receded; Strand opened her eyes and recognized Nelson's parlour, edged with twilight beyond the beam of the stark lamp focused on her. Strand, lying on her stomach on the waist high massage table, struggled to let go of the memory and the fear inside of it.

"Sorry. I was just remembering something, she said raising slightly."

"You want to sit up a minute."

"No, let's just keep going."

He held out her glass with its bent straw and green liquid. She shook her head and started to lower herself back down into the slot meant to cradle her head. Then Strand raised herself on her elbows and gazed at Nelson's heavily laden shelves overflowing with books on painting and drawing that masked the books on history and politics hidden behind them.

"I go. You stay still." Nelson rubbed his dark head, shaved to a gleaming dome, then balanced his thick frame between the heels and balls of his feet. He kept his considerable weight centered so he barely leaned forward over the expanse of Strand's back. For 11 months they'd spent hours in this way: Strand listening to the past unreeling in her head as Nelson worked on her. Other times they'd told each other stories, true and untrue. Under the spell of their words the tattoo took shape almost independently. Now, as they neared the end of the project both were increasingly anxious. Conversation came in choppy swells, uneven and unfinished, without the certainty Strand enforced in most of her life.

"What're you thinking about?"

"Work," Strand lied.

Nelson had grown to expect unpredictability in the flow of Strand's conversation.

"And?"

Strand pushed the shadow back and cast about for news to share: "Did I tell you about the dancing potato chip guy? If I ever have another client like him, I'll leap from a Tower window before we're done."

"They don't open," Nelson responded, never letting his gaze waver from her back.

"Then I'll smash it."

"You don't like heights."

"I won't know, will I?"

"It'd be messy. Your secretary, Freda, would have to clean up after you."

"You want to hear or not," she continued. The hum of Nelson's machine and its vibrating needles remained steady. "He had the stupidest concept I've ever heard. These actors dressed like potato slices hoofing it around the edge of a volcano, like they're about to hop in and get fried."

"Please don't make me laugh, ok?"

"But the thing was he kept insisting we go on location. He wanted to go out West! I said Mount St. Helens is no joke and I wasn't balancing some dumb and desperate dancers on the edge of a volcano when I could do it in a simroom."

"Bet Broadcast loved him."

"He had this deep voice; he kept throwing it around like it was a police stick. 'You don't understand,' he says to me...to me, 'this isn't about your artistic timidity, this is government advertising in Society City."

Nelson tried to hold steady and not laugh at Strand's imitation.

"So, I say, 'No, this is advertising on the far coast and I won't go!' I dumped the job. I couldn't work with this moron. He's had one creative thought in his entire life and this was it."

"Damn Strand, you're rough." Nelson's critique was mixed with admiration.

"There are plenty of other commercialists at the company hungry for the work. Why waste my time with dancing potato chips?"

"Strand." Nelson said, trying to keep the judgment out of his voice, disliking this brittle side of her.

"Broadcast doesn't really like to go past the Cities anyway. And I didn't want to risk my life wandering past the Rockies for some adman! So, end of story, right? Uh uh, today Freda said somebody in Tech told her this guy did end up going out there. I don't know if he got as far as Washington, but out he goes with a crew, you know."

Strains of laughter began to bubble up from her stomach.

"OK, I can feel a break coming on," Nelson stepped back and let his machine arm rest at his side.

"So, he sets off, right, with a crew...I'm sorry." Strand was almost enveloped in laughter. "...he goes out there...forest...unpaved...the whole untamed nature thing and..." Strand raised herself up on her elbows, "and...he gets himself killed!" Her laughter pealed like a bell

"Killed, how?" A chill crossed Nelson's skin.

"Who knows? One of the tech crew said Separatists probably booby trapped the location. They found him practically disemboweled in some woods..."

"That's not funny, Strand."

"Shit, he was an adman."

"And they haven't called themselves Separatists in decades. They're Partisans. Why do they get blamed for everything?"

"Relax."

"You relax!" Nelson snapped, surprised by his impatience. "Don't dismiss people so easily."

"He was just..."

4

"He was just a person."

Both were quiet, an unnatural state between them, until Nelson spoke.

"They keep telling us Partisans are raving lunatics, ready to kill anybody outside the perimeters of the Cities. Why, Strand? Why is the City trying so hard to keep us away from the old places. Away from people trying to hang on to some...some..." he sputtered to the end.

Strand had never heard Nelson so upset, certainly not with her. His cocoa coloured skin was almost flushed with angry red.

"Think Strand! That's supposed to be your claim to fame."

She stared at his books, not seeing their titles. At Broadcast One there was an endless static of voices-- technicians, producers, advertisers, directors like herself. She'd learned to let clients babble while she thought about their concepts, examining them from all angles until she perceived the image she wanted. Then she matched the rhythms and tone of the conversation, pitching her voice above it and off center just enough to capture their attention. As she waited for the space to step in her face looked much as it did now: a store shuttered and closed for the night.

Strand had once caught herself in the glass window of her tower office, that look reflected back, superimposed on the small world below, her mouth set in a hard line which she never broke until a client hired her. For her thoughts, her ideas.

"I correct myself. Don't think. Feel, Strand."

She leaned up for the glass of tranq, sipped and lowered herself back to the table. When Nelson clicked the machine back on, she shuddered, and drifted away from his words. She was afraid to think or feel right now. Instead, she savored the image of him hovering over her body just like he did over his canvas when he worked in the requisite art class they took together. She enjoyed the small island each easel created and the hushed atmosphere of concentration. The tranq floated her away from anxiety.

In class Cardarelli, the instructor, whispered apologetically when she made suggestions over a painter's shoulder, moving about the room, always avoiding Strand who openly resented interruption. She took the class, as required by Professional Development, but PD couldn't make her listen to an instructor if she chose otherwise. With merely a glance Strand was able to decipher, analyze or reproduce any image put before her. She hadn't needed instruction in art since she'd left the orphanage at 15.

"I'm taking a stretch break," Nelson said after a few moments, flipping the switch on the machine. "You want something?"

"No. How much longer do you think?"

"A month, maybe. I'm doing a second layer of colors now."

"It's like we've known each other forever, you know that."

"Except we keep knowing something new."

"Um."

"How's Lynx doing?"

"Good. A lot better, really." Strand thought about

what that meant: Lynx was able to sleep without drugs. She could be in a room with more than one person without the usual sedatives.

"I want her to come by soon."

"She will; it's just hard for her when she gets off her shift."

"Soon, though." Nelson splayed his palms together, pushing and flexing. He brushed her forehead gently with his fingertips then dropped forward at the waist, his large bulk in its dark tee shirt and harem pants filling the space beside Strand. He stretched noisily and squatted by her, his brown face even with hers. His large dark eyes and sleekly arched eyebrows were accentuated by the stark beauty of his bald head.

"You know I'm going to miss you when we're done," he said, and was startled to see tears forming in the corner of her eyes. He turned away, gripped the edge of the table and did two half push-ups.

"Hell, you'll be happy to have more time to hang out at Ruby's and pick up lithe, young men." she replied tartly. Then, more softly as if barely saying it made it barely true, "You and Lynx are the only people in the world I love."

"There'll soon be a lot more."

"If they don't stop us." It was unusual for Strand to express uncertainty.

"They think it's just an art project. They won't care."

"They care about everything, Nelson—the trains running on time and real tattoos."

Working at Broadcast Strand saw how closely the government monitored every nuance of public social interaction from the rare but unquenchable street crime to who bought 'adult' music. Strand didn't underestimate the Society's investment in any of its citizens.

"The Joneses,'" Nelson said with disgust.

The "Joneses" was Nelson's epithet for the Society and its privatized bureaucracy. The federal government was composed of intricately linked, regional oversight committees, really corporations, with profit and order in mind. Since the turn of the last century the Atlantic Union kept obscured but iron-like control over citizen activities after what they called the Great Decline, a series of precipitous events: a deadly virus which reduced the population of the U.S. by thirty percent, then the Pacific States seceded from the Union and the 'Dry Spell,' as Broadcast called it, killed off most farming and living in the Central States. Religion and Business and Government became one for the 'good' of the Union. They strategized how many workers needed education, which citizens had run out of their right to public assistance and would be pressed into public work shifts, which types of artists needed stimulation, or which reproducers needed more books; and, most importantly, which media executives and directors said what over the national channels and streams. Immigration was totally halted and in the largest social engineering project in history citizens in different ethnic groups were 'encouraged' to intermarry in an effort to dispel ethnic solidarity. Outspoken dissidents were said to have 'emigrated,' but they never sent post cards. The Joneses were like an eye in the sky, emitting rays of control—some obvious, most more insidious.

"Back to work if you can stand it."

"I'm just imagining we're in Cardarelli's studio class and I'm the canvas."

Nelson rubbed his hands vigorously around his smooth head as if gathering the thoughts that were inside; then he took the machine in hand. Pinned to the walls around them were the drawings he'd done in Cardarelli's class of Lynx; and others he'd done of Strand over the six

years they'd known each other. He was always looking for the life behind the images. With this tattoo, he'd found it.

Strand herself was usually more interested in affect, her meticulous eye taking in content only tangentially. During her years living in the Society North Orphanage, Strand had learned to watch the shapes of things to discern meaning. The floor supervisor's arched eyebrow let her know what was safe to say. The angle of the door to the Principal's office informed her of how severe her punishment would be. A child's curving lip said she'd refuse to talk to the tall, awkward Strand. A sly look from a boy telegraphed his intent to attempt to abuse her. The act of deciphering these signs became its own meaning; whatever occurred subsequently had been almost inconsequential to the child Strand. She'd lived for symbols and surfaces until two years ago when Lynx arrived to model for their class:

#Lynx stepped up onto the platform, a large crocheted hat crowning her nudity. Kneeling ceremoniously, she drew the hat back from her forehead, releasing a mass of tawny orange hair,

9

emblazoned with streaks of pure silver, to cascade down her back and around her breasts. A collective gasp swept around the studio as

they recognized the silver marks of an empath. Cardarelli beamed with pride. She was the first instructor at the Institute, in the entire city, to have secured an empath as a model. Most of the students had never met one, although they'd certainly heard of the social services performed by the E Corps for the Society in hospitals and detention centers.

Strand forced herself to look away from the mesmerizing tangle of hair, as if it were the lethal locks of Medusa. Strand focused instead on the body, just as she did with clients when their voices got in her way. This one was short, athletic, the arms firm with muscle, a body altogether at odds with the mass of bright, delicate tendrils of hair. The skin, unexpectedly, was not just freckled but bronzed from the sun. Despite the fine bones, her hands looked like those of a toiler, bearers of many heavy loads. Everything about Lynx seemed both small and large at the same time. The set of mismatched attributes was puzzling to Strand. Even in recline Lynx seemed to fill the room.

Strand didn't begin to look at Lynx's face until the end of the fourth class. She spent all her time trying to read her body: the flare of hip from her waist, the texture of skin and the fine hairs that covered it. Near the end of the week Strand realized that Lynx, unlike most models, sat perfectly still. The curve of her muscle was stony hard beneath the flesh. For hours she sat, as if all life were suspended. The only movement was that of her hair, blown occasionally by a current

from the forced air vent. Strand became curious about the concentration at the center of the adamantine stillness. There were no clues in Lynx's face. Her features remained impassive; the bright hazel of her eyes almost opaque. The shield masking Lynx's gaze annoyed Strand at first. Her job was about surfaces, but here she wanted to know the interior image, the hidden meanings.

After class Strand asked Nelson, "So what do you make of her?"

He raised his eyebrows, his fleshy brown face creased with a wide smile. In their years of friendship Strand had never revealed curiosity about anyone. Except him. Her other personal relationships were brief, ephemeral, significant only when they were discarded—material to dissect over dinner and wine.

"Girlfriend, I know what you know. She's mother nature's creature, but not one I've ever seen before."

"Empath."

""I got the silver hair thing," Nelson answered impatiently. "But she

never moves. Shit's racing around inside there, though. You know?"

"Um."

"I've seen her a couple of times at Ruby's, always with the hat, though."

"Why would she go to that greasy spoon?"

"Why would I go? To eat some greens, to look at folks and keep the

Joneses from keeping up with you."

"Ruby's?"

"Yeah." Nelson worked hard to sound as noncommittal as Strand.

"See you tomorrow," Strand had said, walking away, not sure herself what thoughts she hid.

"Earth to Strand." Nelson said when he realized Strand had fallen asleep on the table. "Where do you go in there? You were out for the count."

She sat up quickly, startled. "Let's go light on the tranq next time, whew!"

"Sometimes I wish I could hook up some speakers to that brain of yours."

"What! So, you can fall asleep too!" Strand laughed as he helped her down from the table.

He sprayed a thin layer of the surgical fixative then handed Strand, ever distrustful of DuPont, one of the oversized tee shirts she now wore beneath all of her clothes. He watched her drape it as gently as he did his easel. He avoided touching her back as they embraced, smiling at the soft texture of her hair.

"Tomorrow and tomorrow and tomorrow. Isn't that some movie?"

The sparkle in Strand's eyes concealed whether she thought she was joking or not. Nelson held the intercom open so she could hear him still laughing down in the lobby and out into the courtyard.

Back in her own flat, Strand sipped a tall glass of water, hoping to hurry the tranquilizer from her system. She never slept until Lynx rang the phone once to signal she was home. If she let it ring more than once they'd talk. Strand lay across the bed; when the phone rang for the third time, she pressed the button in the bed's headboard.

"Hello, I hope it's not too late." Lynx's voice still carried the soft curve of the non-city dweller.

"Hi, I just got home from Nelson's."

"Did you two have a good time?"

A ray of amusement glinted through the awkward necessity of sounding casual. The Jones' randomly listened to telephone conversations in the housing complex.

"Great," Strand answered. "He's a wonderful artist." Her belief in the praise was undisguised.

"Have you eaten?" Lynx asked.

"I'm too beat."

"I'll let you go then. I just wanted to...to get in touch."

"Thanks, let's get together soon." Strand became impatient with the form they followed so cautiously.

"Wonderful. I was hoping you'd be open." A smile suffused Lynx's voice.

"What about tomorrow?"

"Perfect, I have a new piece I'd like to show you." Lynx barely suppressed laughter.

Strand clicked off and lay back down. In the last year and a half, she and Lynx had kept their relationship quiet, rarely going out as a couple. Only when they were together in one of their flats did they allow their need for each other to spill out in words and touch. For months it had been like a game they played: tricking the Joneses. Now it was a tight band around Strand's chest squeezing her breath, smothering her. But Lynx's attempts at erotic humor made her smile. *She sounded weary*, Strand thought as she plummeted into sleep.

SESSION #82

"What," Strand said without looking away from her monitor. She'd shifted light and color on the brand new sedan for the past hour and nothing made it appealing, unusual, or seem like a necessity. When Freda didn't answer Strand looked away from the screen in frustration, "What is it?"

Freda, secretary on Strand's floor for almost 5 years, stood tentatively in the doorway. The intelligence in her eyes was sometimes shadowed by the stress of working in advertising but more often by her inability to comprehend Strand. Freda's mind and her short, round body moved with equal dexterity around the political potholes of Broadcast One, and she knew she was one of the reasons Strand had a successful career. But it was never clear how Strand felt about this.

"I talked to Dee, in the pool. She's got those contracts covered. I'm going..."

"What about Dee?" Strand said still unable to focus on her secretary.

"She's going to finish those contracts you just gave me. Remember, I have my videography class tonight." Freda's voice was still threaded with a light accent that Strand assumed was from Puerto Rico, but she'd never inquired.

"Dee can't do this, Freda. I need you on this one. We're using too many specialists on this shoot; everyone has a contract. I've got to have it first thing in the morning--done right."

"Dee's good, Strand. I've got her set up and I'll log in and check her work after my class."

"Then what? If she fucks up, I'm screwed."

"If there are mistakes, I'll have time..."

"Freda, do you work for me or not?" Strand turned back to the monitor, stared at the wash of red and began to calibrate its intensity. "I'm leaving here at seven."

Freda bit back a reply and tried to keep in mind the exhilaration she felt when Strand and she talked about a successful video shoot. She shut the door to Strand's office quietly and returned to her desk.

When Strand swung through the pool to leave at 7:15, Freda raised the stack of contracts with a trim smile.

"I always tell them you're the best, Freda!" Strand said as she pressed the elevator button.

At Nelson's house Strand stepped out of her clothes with the same ease with which she'd forgotten the exchange with Freda. Nelson inspected his mix of colors and the needle machine, as Strand laid her pants and tunic neatly on the back of an overstuffed reading chair Nelson had rescued from a theatre where he'd designed a set. Gazing into an ornate mirror over the couch, she thought she looked fuller without her clothes. The slowing metabolism of her middle years was revealed in her hips and thighs. Tonight, the thickening made her smile.

15

"Any ripples outside?" Nelson asked.

"No," Strand tried to dismiss the increasing unease she'd felt over the past few weeks.

"I'm just gonna go back to do a few lines. I don't want to work too long."

"Up or down?" she asked.

"Down."

Strand stretched out on her stomach with a sigh.

"Sometimes the work just comes, like squeezed out of a tube. Other times I can't hook in. Does that make sense?"

"It's taking longer than you thought."

Nelson turned his attention to a line on Strand's thigh.

"We'll all get together soon.

"Good idea."

"Remember that first time?"

"Uh huh."

"I'll never be that way again, will I, Nelson?"

He raised the machine. "No, I don't think so."

Then he was immersed in the work, his breathing in tune with the machine and its vibrating needles. Strand strained upward to look at the natural lines he drew on her thighs, the ink perfectly distributed, blood welling around it. She closed her eyes and tried to remember the moment the change had begun.

#The entire class had worked intently at their easels. Strand avoided meeting Nelson's eyes for a smile as they occasionally did. Just before the session ended, she pushed her easel to the edge of the studio, then slipped out.

16

On the street instinct took over as it did when she worked. Pictures were what guided her. The image of Ruby's drew her: a narrow, brick structure on the edge of the city, with a brightly-lit window where they served messy food to people who stayed far into the night. She'd had dinner there once with Nelson and some of his friends from his housing block, all the while unnerved by the noise and aimlessly circular discussions. She imagined the entire place to be under the shadow of a brown cloud, the effluvia of frying foods and overlong bantering. She kept going even though a puckering distaste filled her mouth.

Watching through a window of the rumbling jitney, she recognized the long, brightly-lit window as they passed, but stayed on board for several more blocks to get a clearer sense of the neighborhood. She leapt out in front of the darkened facade of a beauty salon and made her way back to Ruby's entrance. She stood between the double set of glass doors. At first, she saw only her own reflection—tall, unyielding posture accentuated by the spare lines of her fullsuit which hugged the curves of her body. Her skin, the shade of golden oak, was unlined at the age of 40. The tight row of braids curving around the crown of her head was accurately austere, threaded with gray. She appreciated the image without smiling.

Behind her the sound of laughter and shouted food orders floated through the cafe. She shifted her gaze; looking out through the glass more intently than she'd ever looked at anything other than a studio set. She wondered what she'd do if Lynx didn't recognize her.

17

The muted green of the crocheted cap alerted Strand as Lynx came down the street toward the cafe. Strand pulled the door open just as Lynx stood before it. She brushed hesitancy aside and said 'Surprise' in the lightest voice she could muster. A cloud lifted from the ice of Lynx's eyes, which lightened almost to amber as she laughed. She tried to say Strand's name but couldn't stop laughing. Strand only stared as Lynx's laughter rolled from her uncontrollable. The hidden catch broken, mirth enveloped Lynx so totally it was alarming. Lynx grabbed Strand's arm as if to stop herself from falling.

"Let me hold on, please, just a moment. Please," she said between eruptions. Strand watched steadily, not understanding what it meant, regretting she'd followed her impulse. Lynx's grip began to bruise her arm. The color in Lynx's eyes darkened as she felt Strand's pain and the laughter stopped. She let go of Strand, wiping tears from the corners of her eyes.

"I just wanted..." the words strangled each other in Strand's throat. "I startled you."

Lynx smiled. "It happens so rarely. I'm sorry I frightened you."

"You didn't."

"Yes. I did. And I am sorry. I'll never become used to living among people." Lynx's voice was only partly playful.

"Yeah, I know what you mean."

"Yes, you do." Lynx's eyes narrowed as she peered at Strand. "You're the one in the figure class."

"Strand."

"Yes." The sibilants slipped from Lynx's mouth like taffy—slow, intriguing.

"I was just leaving."

"Oh?" Lynx was puzzled at the lie she could feel all around them.

Noise filled Strand's ears, blocking out Lynx's voice. She took a deep breath and caught the soft scent of soap. "Excuse me," Strand said coolly then stepped around Lynx, escaping through the doors.

Strand shifted on the table, thinking about that first time; her old discomfort with Lynx felt alien now.

"OK, sisterlove, that's it for tonight." Nelson's voice broke into her thoughts. "I got the right perspective. Finally! It's going to be perfect."

He sprayed ceremoniously.

"Don't look, come on now, don't look. You can't see anything anyhow!"

Uncharacteristically obedient, Strand didn't try to examine the work. Instead, she turned sideways in the ornate mirror and admired the small tattoo of an old-fashioned bicycle on her calf--a large spoked wheel with a much smaller one behind.

"What'd you call this again?"

"A penny-farthing." Nelson had done it in the first year of their friendship saying: "It'll take you anywhere you want to go." He started cleaning up his instruments. "If anybody asks, we were sketching..." he trailed off, thinking, "...kitchen utensils and what was his name... kind of doodling but scary, was he 20th century?"

"Basquiat!" Strand provided their alibi with a laugh.

" Aha!" Nelson said, then, "Don't be letting nobody be patting you."

"Yes, I know, I know."

At the end of every session the project seemed riskier than the day before. The Society didn't care for the renegade art of tattooing any more than it did for travel to the West. Laws had first restricted the art in the 19th century. Now, more than two hundred and fifty years later, the laws were unequivocal. Nelson felt like the proprietor of one of the needle parlours he'd read about in his historical novels, in which squalid back rooms dotted the waterfront, catering to drunken seamen.

Strand left Nelson's studio a little dazed as the drug wore off and the pain of the needles reached her. It'd been over a year since she and Lynx had become lovers, something else the Society would frown on—workers were meant to stay in their own circles. And certainly no one was supposed to become lovers with a government empath. She hurried toward Lynx's room, a small loft space looking out over a factory loading dock. All along the way she felt that prickly sensation that someone was watching her. She turned several times and thought she saw a shadowy figure but nothing was too in focus after a session on the tattoo table. Finally she let herself in, rubbed Lynx's cat and dog in response to their eager greetings, wondering how they decided who to like and who to snub. Few people had permission from the medical providers to keep pets in the Society so it was a little strange to Strand to have small, living things moving around her.

She lay on her stomach across the bed where the cat and dog circled after they finished eating. She didn't move at the sound of Lynx's step on the stairs, only listened, feeling her body come alive with the waiting.

Lynx hummed as she entered her room, lowered herself to the bed and cautiously pulled the shirt over Strand's head. The waves of her hair were tied back in a white ribbon. Her uniform was rumpled and stained with hours of sweat. She kissed one of the parts in Strand's hair and without speaking massaged Strand's head, running her strong fingers along the rows of braids. They were a pale shade of blue this week, dyed to match an outfit she'd worn for a film premiere. Strand and Nelson had made a striking pair in twin outfits. High visibility meant more jobs. Tired of finding scarves to match, Strand swore that before the weekend her hair would be its usual silver-flecked brown again.

Lynx worked her way down Strand's neck and shoulders, massaging the air above her muscles gently. Soon Strand felt the heat of Lynx's hands as they passed above the raw lines where Nelson had been working. Lynx held her palms just over the solid edges and the wash of bronze and silver that he'd created on Strand's back. Lynx's breath quickened and she resisted drawing away the wound completely--taking in all the pain risked the durability of the picture. She drew out a portion of the burning, pulling it into herself and releasing it into the air. She worked quickly, anxious to be done with the healing and to feel Strand's body more intimately.

21

The lines that lay across and down Strand's back were intriguingly familiar to Lynx. Even unfinished, they began to take shape and open themselves to her. As Lynx worked, Strand wondered how they'd feel when the tattoo was done, and a shiver of fear rippled across her skin. Lynx held her hand steady continuing to trace the outline of pale color making Strand's skin first warm then cool.

"How did it go today?"

"Nelson is pleased. He says I have good legs. Soon they'll be twice as good." Strand smiled, but Lynx did not.

"Earlier, when I was at the hospital, I was resting between patients and I closed my eyes. I saw blood. Spilling down your flesh."

"At the beginning I tried to watch Nelson working."

"Tried?"

"I didn't watch long. Not like me, being squeamish, is it?"

"Not like you at all, Strand."

"Do you want us to stop?"

"It's a bit like dying. I've felt that with patients, you know. A loosening inside myself."

"Should we stop?"

"No."

The muscles in Strand's body relaxed. The heat now emanating from her body was not from the wounds. Lynx touched the inside of Strand's thigh lightly, then entered her from behind.

While they waited for the sedative to take effect, Nelson showed Strand one of his old books, its pages wrinkled and soft. The pictures from the early 1900s showed men and women with primitive tattoos covering most of their bodies: flowery hearts, battleships, flags. Other pages reproduced the more sophisticated tattoos of indigenous people from some of the lost Pacific Islands. The tight lines and bands were so compelling Strand knew the project was the right thing to do. She began disrobing, looking at the bric-a-brac which crowded Nelson's shelves.

"What's this little car?"

"Isn't it great? See those wheels? White wall tires, fabulous!" Nelson plucked the replica of the antique Stutz Bearcat from his book shelf. Its trim design was solid in his hand. "This was a real car. My grandfather used to say he knew western civilization was doomed when

all the cars started looking just alike. Alfa Romeo, Mercedes, Cadillac, Jag, Saab, Mustang--by the turn of the century the designs were interchangeable."

"He could have been right," Strand said. The pleasure Nelson took in his memories of his family pleased her, even though she had none of her own. Each session was an interior journey for them both. They exchanged history and ideas with an urgency and intimacy few citizens bothered with in Society City. At the same time Strand heard Nelson's stories or told her own she was traveling away from everything she knew about herself, to a destination she couldn't yet picture in her mind.

She climbed onto the table, relinquishing her body to Nelson's hand. The light markings he made as a guide tickled her skin.

"I'm going back to the right shoulder today. Warn me if you need to stop. But no fidgeting."

"I'll be fine."

"Yeah, I know you're tough. But don't wait 'til you're ready to leap from the table before you say 'white flag,' OK?

Strand slipped easily under the spell of the high-pitched hum of the needle. The first touch was like a small bite, then the sensation radiated out in dull waves of stimulation. Nelson told her that traditional tattoo artists hadn't used tranquilizers. She didn't see why he insisted she take them, yet the vivid memories it induced usually pleased her.

#On the final day of the figure drawing cycle, the end of Lynx's work as their model, Nelson had cajoled Strand into having a drink with him at Ruby's Cafe. He returned waves and shouts from other customers as they took a table by the windows. Within minutes of ordering drinks, Nelson leapt from his seat and dashed to the front where Lynx stood hesitantly inside the glass double doors. She smiled when she saw Nelson. Strand felt annoyed and trapped as Nelson and Lynx headed back to the table.

After eight weeks of art class Nelson and Strand were the only two willing to acknowledge Lynx; everyone else fled as if she would read their minds for sport. After her first misstep at the restaurant door Strand had never managed more than a studied 'hello' every session; but that was more than the rest of the workshop participants. For the next half hour, the din of Ruby's swirled around them while they endured stilted attempts at conversation: about the drawing they'd seen in the studio class, about Professional Development, and about the neighborhood. The owner, Ruby, was behind the bar--six feet tall, dark skin and sloe-eyed, commanding the room even when she was just washing the glasses. She brought a bottle of wine and refilled their glasses without being called, greeting Nelson familiarly.

"You're not switching on me, are ya?" she asked, smiling at Lynx and Strand.

"Not yet. Lynx, Strand, this is the inestimable Ruby."

"He promised I'm first if he gets the urge."

"And who was it that was gonna protect me from Danny?"

"When I finished with you, sweetie, you'd need hospital rest anyway." Ruby's laughter filled the restaurant as she went back to the bar.

Strand watched, puzzled; she didn't realize Nelson was such a regular at Ruby's. When they ate dinner out it was usually in their own part of town, near the complex. As Ruby's laughter trailed off, Lynx spoke: "Will you tell me about tattoos?"

Nelson hesitated only a moment before breaking into a smile which Strand recognized as his preface to a story. Strand was surprised again, this time at his open enthusiasm since neither of them was sure where empaths stood precisely in the Jones family tree.

"It's fine to talk with me," Lynx answered the unspoken question and lightly rested her freckled hand on Strand's arm. A comforting sensation pulsed through Lynx's fingers to Strand. Nelson began to tell her some of the history of body adornment, about his books, the lore.

"They tattooed something they thought they needed; even when it was just boasting, it was still wishful thinking. Even in the tiniest rose resting on someone's hip bone I saw yearning, urgency like nothing in the galleries."

"I was looking for the images that filled me up, not just paint on paper. When I did my first tattoo, I knew I had it." He looked closely for Lynx's reaction before he went on.

"The purr of the electricity is exciting. When the needles prick flesh, I almost feel it. The entering, the connecting are exhilarating. And then there's the picture, eternal in a mortal kind of way."

"I don't know if I could bear the intrusion," Lynx said.

"It's not for everybody. You got to understand the meaning of taking on an image. Taking that image inside yourself. Once you do you can stand anything, I think."

Lynx smiled at Nelson and Strand watched her intently.

"Hey, I don't want you two to think this is a set up, but I'm out of here." Nelson fumbled under the table for his case, at the same time looking toward the door.

"What?" Strand said, her annoyance escalating to anger.

"Sorry, I've got a late date."

Strand stared coldly at him, then at the smiling man standing in the doorway.

"Don't give me that look, girlfriend. Be sociable, I'm going to be."

Nelson pulled his long, full sweater from the back of the chair.

"See ya, right?" he smiled at Lynx.

"I hope so."

"My treat." He waved at them in the mirror and paid Ruby at the bar before sweeping out the door.

"I apologize. Nelson doesn't usually make a fool of himself in front of people, especially over men."

"No need. I hoped we'd get the chance to talk."

Strand thought about the tone and shape of Lynx's voice. The elongated vowels made it seem as if she were speaking with great deliberation, thinking in another language. Lynx sat almost as still as she did in class, waiting. They sipped the rest of their drinks in silence.

"What was it like growing up...being an empath?" Strand finally asked, reaching for her training in social manners. The shadow which crossed Lynx's face made Strand regret her inquiry. Lynx spoke quickly, her voice low and hoarse.

"My mother, Mae, figured I was weak. Melancholy too, I guess. She's a plain woman. Not much for cities or books. She must have thought that empaths were somebody the Society made up, like hobgoblins. Frankensteins they cooked up in labs or something."

Lynx laughed when Strand looked puzzled. "Monsters, men made up out different body parts."

27

"Ugh!"

"As I got older Mae just thought I was mad. And I was, for a while."

Lynx looked around the room as if others might have heard her last words. But the music from the old stereo speakers still washed over the rise and fall of conversation, the clink of dishes and glassware. Ruby's was one of the few places individuals didn't submit to tiny speakers in their ears. She liked everyone to experience the same music and sound together. Its noise shielded Lynx from the crowd but it could not protect her. The exultation of a woman and man—bathed in desire, sitting impatiently at a back table—radiated across the room. The cold fury of a young woman sitting at the counter pierced Lynx's skin. Their waiter's exhaustion, as he set down their drinks, sapped her strength.

"I can feel all of it, the deepest things they feel. Him, her, them," she said, nodding her head around the room. "Swirling inside me. Back then I thought I was possessed. I couldn't escape, and I couldn't explain what was happening."

"Children from the farms nearby made fun of me when they saw me sitting with our cows in the pasture instead of going to school. Their parents pointed at me and followed me around whenever I went to town. Why do people think experiencing curiosity automatically

gives them the right to your life?"

The urgency in Lynx's voice made Strand want to touch her. Lynx took a breath and went on.

"Then my hair began to change. The silver ate through

the red and for the first time I really loved something about myself. I didn't care who stared. Mae used to brush it every night for the longest time. But I could feel her fear. Then they came and took me away."

The words alarmed Strand, who'd never paid much attention to who empaths were, where they'd come from or how they served society. In that moment, she felt a part of the "they" who'd come to snatch Lynx from her home. One of the Jones'.

"I was tranquilized for a year. Therapists did exercises with my body, they fed me intravenously most of that time. Control voices were played almost constantly on implants." Lynx lifted her unusual hair away from her neck and displayed the tiny line where the incision had been made. Strand, with years of practice, easily concealed any obvious reaction.

"It was like living outside my body, a twelve month dream. And when they thought I'd be able to protect myself from the tumult of feeling they took me off the tranqs and started to train me."

"What do you mean 'train'?"

"Most empaths acquire the sensitivity later in life, after we've already learned how to preserve individuality. I was too young and susceptible to everyone. I had to be trained to open and close, to draw in and release the sensations without being subsumed by them."

"The Society doesn't give anything away for free." Strand's suspicions rose.

"Society's correctional hospitals, the health care system, they couldn't function without us. We're their intellectual property, in a manner of speaking."

Pride was new to Lynx. She'd experienced it for the first time when she was able to move inside the pain of another and help untangle it. She maintained a precarious balance between that joy and a sense of being used for purposes she could not know.

"But we have to be supervised, so our health doesn't wear down. I fought to be allowed to live in the city, to work with children, not just with convicted offenders."

"Why here?"

"The training tapes hadn't really worked. I thought I could train myself to be around people in one of the cities. But now I'm either completely closed down, like when I'm modeling for the class, or too open, like when I think of you."

Strand looked from Lynx to her glass, keeping her noncommittal expression in place.

"I feel you so much and I want to know you," Lynx said a crimson flush rising from her neck to her cheeks.

Strand didn't speak but took a sip from her glass.

"I know what you're feeling too. I'm sorry, I can't help it. I know."

"How can you?" Strand said, her voice wavering only slightly. To be known frightened her more than she'd ever admitted to herself.

"I've been trying to explain. I more than know—I feel what you're feeling. You can't hide from me even when you run away like you did that first time. I watched you through the window as you left. I felt the battle inside you."

Strand leaned back from the table as if to leave.

"Don't." Lynx gripped Strand, pressing her hand into the rough wood edge of the tiny table.

"Push away! That was your feeling just then. But you want to sink inside me, too. It's all there coursing through your body. Your facility to keep it bricked up inside is amazing."

Strand looked down at their hands locked together, expecting them to glow with the heat she felt.

"You look at my fingers and want them in your mouth," Lynx said with an edge of wonder. "You want my fingers pressing inside your mouth, you sucking, pulling, tasting."

Strand glared at their hands. Her gaze did not soften as she looked up into Lynx's eyes.

"Why does desire make you want to hurt me? Or is it the knowing?" Then Lynx asked, "Do you want to marry this fear?" She inhaled so deeply it felt impossibly long, then removed her hand.

At the release Strand, at first, felt the weight of abandonment as she'd never experienced before, even on the worst days living in the Society orphanage. Then her breath caught in her chest as if Lynx had been holding her hand over her mouth and nose, stopping the air. She gasped and breathed deeply, her chest heaving.

"I'm going to have to give you another tranq, Strand." Nelson stretched his arms above his head. "You're acting up."

"What?" Strand said, disoriented.

31

"You're starting to thrash around."

She opened her eyes and saw, spread out under her shoulder, the towel spotted with her blood.

"Oh."

"Take this," Nelson said, thrusting the glass of green liquid toward her, its bent plastic straw reaching toward her.

"I'm fine, just a dream."

Nelson's hand was steady, the glass did not retreat.

Strand yielded, ran her tongue over the straw then drew a small amount of the liquid in. She closed her eyes to await the relaxation.

"You've got to be still as stone here, girl. I want not a hair out of place."

"I'm sorry. I drift away, into the past."

"How about talking to me. About anything, as long as you stay still."

Many times, she and Nelson sat together, in bars, parks, telling each other their life stories, being each other's confidant in a way that was more common to adolescents than adults. They'd both come to the capital from small towns in the north, near New Hampshire's border, where the highway leading to Society City was the yellow brick road for anyone who wanted to be an artist. They each had done work which had caught the attention of local councilors early in their careers, and each petitioned and won the opportunity to move to the City.

They'd spied each other one day in the Art Park that was at the center of the housing compound where they lived. Dwelling on opposite ends of a complex of high-rises built explicitly for art workers, they rarely crossed the expanse of regimentally manicured green lawn that sat at its center. It resembled a miniature baseball diamond, but instead of bases there were strategically placed pieces of art, mostly replicas, meant to inspire the residents, some of whom sat sketching or writing in their shadows.

Despite Strand's disdain for the programmed nature of their artistic environment, she'd requested permission to remain in the artists' compound after she began working in advertising and broadcast. One visit to the complexes designed for media professionals and Strand had known they were too shiny and noisy for her. Painting was quiet and the silent typing of writers was less to contend with than the endless static of broadcast voices emptied of their regional shadings. She much preferred the trite Modigliani imitations and Romare Beardon rip-offs which surrounded her to the premieres and festivals that sprawled across the huge screens dominating the media complexes.

The Society liked imitation; perfect replication was as prized as any original. She and Nelson smirked secretly with each other about the imitative nature of the artwork around them. No matter how crowded and tough the city was, neither of them wanted to be sent to some outpost like Chicago to design stamps or traffic signs.

A new Richard Serra replica resembling a rusted flying wedge was installed in the outfield soon after they'd met. Strand came upon Nelson late one night tossing a pair of shoes, tied together by their laces, into the air, trying to land them hanging across the fourteen foot high slab of metal. His drunken state was making his aim unpredictable, so Strand grabbed the shoes and tossed expertly, leaving the muddy size twelves dangling irreverently.

"City kids, poor ones, used to do that all over the country decades ago," he said, laughing.

"Why would poor people throw away their shoes?" she asked, genuinely perplexed.

"Who knows? To leave their mark, to keep being poor from totally dictating their lives?" he shrugged.

Strand pushed herself to imagine that time before the Society corporatized, when children would be allowed to throw away shoes. "Maybe they just wanted to see how high they could throw," she speculated.

They'd been friends ever since.

"Well?" Nelson said, putting down the electric needles he used to insert bright colors under her skin. He rinsed and dried his hands then took up a sketching crayon.

"Tell me how Lynx is doing; be specific."

Strand always felt his inquiries about Lynx were as much about herself as Lynx. "She's having a difficult time controlling the barrage of sensations. She takes the blocking drugs when she has to but they slow her work and numb her for anything else."

"What about that hypnotist I told you about?"

"She ended up hypnotising him."

Nelson would have laughed had he not heard the strain in Strand's voice. "And the acupuncture?"

"That's been a relief sometimes. But when she comes

home, she lies in the dark for hours, like a corpse."

"The Jones' aren't going to let their valuable property go on like that for long."

"The more she opens to me the less strength she has to screen out everyone else. Her supervisor is already insisting she go on blockers all the time. She'll end up immobilised in a hospital with medicos bringing patients to her bedside for healing like she's some kind of ghoul."

"Steady."

Strand concentrated on lying still, then said, "I want to watch you in the mirror."

"Come on, you don't want to do that."

He felt her body stiffen and knew her well enough to recognize her on the edge of fury. So, he pulled over a small table and placed his shaving mirror and another small hand mirror at angles so she could watch him work.

"I'm going back to the leg lines."

Strand watched the arch of Nelson's wrist and felt the soft tip of the pencil on her calves. The grip of his fingers was echoed in the determined set of his lips. It was a look she'd seen often in their art class and on the dance floor.

"You talk."

A shiver went through her when he picked up the needle. *Such a primordial custom,* she thought. *Funny how it had lasted so long despite attempts to outlaw it.* So many citizens had a tattoo or two or three, most created by the pencils which were quick and relatively painless. The ink was designed to wear off in several months.

Strand felt the muted sting of the needle on the back of her leg and watched the blood rise in the track behind the needle. The line extending up her calf to her thigh was fascinating to her, as if she were reading her palm. Nelson worked with steady deliberation, his eyes never leaving the line. She couldn't see the colour of the dye, only the dark red which sometimes welled up and slipped down the side of her leg. She felt curiously ill for a moment and sniffed in surprise.

"You alright?"

"I was just thinking..."

"Please, no thinking. Talk."

"I'm not certain how you expect me to do the latter without the former."

"Chatter is good for the soul."

Strand closed her eyes. "We finally got permission for our trip to the country, for a week. Soon."

She waited for Nelson to get to the end of a line and lift his head.

"It's not my favourite thing to do in the middle of a piece, but I guess it's time."

"Her mother still feels guilty letting them take her."

"What's to feel guilty about? When the Jones' want to take you away that's what they do. Mother or no mother." His voice deepened with emotion.

"Maybe when she sees us together, she'll know it's for the best.

And Lynx can see the farm animals she loves."

Strand was quiet as Nelson set to work again. Strand knew that growing up with livestock had made it easy for Lynx to gain permission to have familiars when she moved to the city. She also understood why most people living in cities disapproved of keeping animals. But from the beginning Nelson had never said anything negative about it. A few citizens kept licensed service animals for assorted physical, emotional or mental needs but it was still unusually. After she'd seen Lynx with them—the thin, dark dog called Sliver and the fat black and white fur ball of a cat called Dot scampering in to be with Lynx when she needed them –Strand had accepted it. She was even looking forward to seeing a live cow.

"Quiet for a minute while I get this last bit." She could feel Nelson thinking.

"Alright," he said after a few moments of work. "That's it for the
    time being. I'd let that heal some on its own before I'd do a lot of sitting."

Strand laughed at the maternal timbre of his voice and slipped into her oversized shirt and loose pants. She missed the one-piece simplicity of her fullsuit, but was beginning to enjoy the sensation of the soft folds of fabric brushing her skin as she moved.

By the time she was back in her own high rise apartment the dulling effect of the tranq was thinning and Strand was hungry. She ignored the beep of her mail box and started dinner. Lynx was on duty at the correctional hospital and wouldn't call until later. Strand wanted to have eaten and gotten comfortable by then; this was a night they'd get to talk. Looking at the perfectly balanced picture her dinner plate made, she laughed at her own obsession with visual presentation, then deliberately swirled the food around into a mess.

Strand stood in front of the mail screen with her dinner and clicked on her messages as she began to eat. The word OVERRIDE filled the square of light, then the message:

> TO: <smb@art.pro.res> Strand Maria Burroughs
> Your presence is required tomorrow at 9 am in the office of the Deputy Director of Social Security. This office is located on the 4th floor of the Society City Bureau on Broadway and Main Street. Please be prompt. Expect to remain for a period of 2 hours. Areas of discussion: Artists' Compound, Constructive social contacts. Your employer, Broadcast One, has been informed of this required absence."

Strand hit the print button just to be certain it was as she'd read it on the screen. As the printer spooled and reproduced the message, she dumped her food in the disposal and filled a glass with white wine. She read the message again, the paper trembling in her hand.

Her living room was not especially large, but its picture window facing the city skyline made it feel cavernous at night. Strand paced in front of the backdrop of twinkling lights, oblivious to all except the piece of paper in her hand. She peered at the places where she knew the computer program had dropped the particulars of the message into the form: her name, her employer's name, time, areas of discussion. *Constructive social contacts*. That could mean anything. But they'd said *Artists' Compound*. It must be

38

something about her and Nelson.

The phone rang.

"Yes?"

"What is it?" Lynx said after a breath of hesitation.

"I'll meet you at the mirrors when you're done."

"Now." Lynx broke the connection immediately.

Strand hurriedly typed a message to Nelson: "I hope you found the note I left. See you tomorrow. SMB." Strand had been almost certain they'd never have to use this prearranged warning and as she hit SEND the message seemed both ominous and silly.

It was logical that someone would find out about the tattoo eventually; questions would be raised. The Society was benevolent but only to a point. The intersection of kind concern and control was located wherever any event occurred which the Jones' didn't understand, or which could be construed as disruptive.

Strand hoped Nelson wouldn't be out all night or forget to check his messages in time to hide his treasured machines. Along with architectural miniatures and toy cars, over the years he'd obtained a collection of antique tattoo irons. If the DSS decided to sweep through, tattoo needles would spark more attention than replicas of old tourist sites.

She slammed out the door and waited impatiently for the elevator,

trying not to let anxiety swallow her. One of Society's ubiquitous jitneys pulled up faster than the elevator had and she stood in front of the mirrored bar at Ruby's before Lynx arrived. The place was eerie at such a late hour, almost lifeless without the noise of a full bar. Ruby greeted her with a smile and poured a glass of the wine she usually drank.

Strand tried not to gulp as she watched through the glass doors. She felt dread as she had the first evening, but this time when she saw Lynx push the double doors open escape was not on her mind. Lynx approached warily, unused to seeing Strand off balance. She read the letter in a glance.

"I don't know what it means," Strand said, her voice almost steady, "but people down at the Department of Social Security are more about security than being social. Assume they know about the tattoo." Her tension was a hard wind against Lynx's skin.

"We have to make the trip to my mother." There was no plea in Lynx's voice.

"I know. They're probably watching us."

"They always watch empaths."

Strand looked out the window, realizing she was almost never out this late. "Sometimes I hate this city. Even being outside is like being inside. Under a roof with everyone spying."

Lynx wanted to reassure Strand but was unsure how to go about it. Stating the facts was what Strand seemed to need right now.

"Every day they get closer to demanding what they really want. I've been trained to slip inside of others, to manipulate what they feel or know in order to heal them. But not everyone can be healed." Lynx's voice was barely a whisper. Strand leaned closer but resisted her desire to touch her arm, to try to protect her.

"I've done things for the Society I can't think about at night. I won't go on, Strand."

"We're almost done." Strand dug deeply for her confidence, but uncertainty clouded her words. "Maybe the three of us should go to your mother's and finish."

"We must stay relaxed, listening. Not exuding."

"What?" Strand leaned on the bar as a picture formed of herself with water spouting from her head or stuffing leaking from her seams.

"It's almost like that." Lynx laughed, reading the picture. "What you feel rolls off of you like waves. Even when you're perfectly still. Remember that tomorrow. If this is serious, they're sure to have an empath there to listen."

"I handle bureaucrats at Broadcast every day."

"Things are different for us now, Strand. Don't concentrate on blocking your feelings like you usually do. Focus on taking in what they're exuding."

The expression on Strand's face didn't change but Lynx could feel her doubt.

"You can do it. Take the concentration you usually use to close yourself off. Reverse it. Don't worry about what they can get from you, listen to them. Listen hard."

Strand felt exposed in the glare of Ruby's lights and glass.

"We better get going," she said. "We'll still do the trip."

Lynx nodded, the tight braid of her bright curls hanging heavily down her back. Strand put her arm

41

around her shoulder as they walked outside, glancing nervously up the street. Once Lynx had boarded a jitney, Strand watched to see if anyone emerged and followed. City lights and pollution made it impossible to see stars. The night was bright and empty. Strand let go of her thoughts and tried to float free, listening to what was in the air. A wall of night sound blurred around her; its almost indecipherable noises buffeting her. She focused outward and let

the night speak. The noise rose to a din. Behind her she heard the soft murmur of thoughts and voices from a window above. She relaxed into listening and could distinguish individuals--a child, two men, a woman alone--floating around her head like cumulus clouds. She began to understand what Lynx lived with every day.

Then Ruby pulled the front door shut behind her with an end-of- day-finality and Strand remembered where she was. She hurried home to decide what to wear to her meeting.

The next morning Strand opened the door to the 4th floor office of the Department of Social Security at exactly 9 am. The clean lines of the office had been amplified to austerity: prim chairs were fabricated from some unidentifiable and undoubtedly recycled material, blank walls in varying shades of pale green, no magazines but small popup screens on every table. The receptionist blossomed with good cheer despite the hour and her surroundings. The Department of Social Security, the largest of the government's privately run agencies, kept track of all the citizens and their financial status, making certain they paid taxes and traffic tickets. It monitored who studied what disciplines to be certain the market wasn't glutted; who married whom to keep pace with population growth; and who lived where, to be certain neighbourhoods were developed symmetrically. All was accomplished with a congenial smile and decrees that had no court of appeal. Citizens felt secure and most had easily forgotten privacy. Freedom came through careful management of the population and early elimination of potential trouble spots.

Strand was feeling like one of those spots when two people in matching green suits looked up at her as the receptionist showed her into the office.

"Burroughs, thank you for joining us," said the man. "I'm Skinner and this is McKinnon."

"How do you do Doctor. Professor," Strand replied in her best orphanage-trained voice. She recognised Skinner as an author of some of the theories in which the Society was grounded. Strand knew McKinnon had written somewhere that the population needed to be protected from itself, its baser instincts. Women, in McKinnon's mind, were especially vulnerable.

Strand watched their bodies. Despite the gender difference they were curiously alike--tight, angular--each suspended in a carefully constructed air of nonchalance. Then she listened. Not especially to what they asked her, but to what they didn't ask and to what they thought of her answers.

"We realise it's early; can we bring you tea or coffee?" McKinnon asked congenially. Strand noticed the perfection of her teeth and how uninflected her voice was, as if she were a television anchor rather than a bureaucrat.

"Yes, thank you." The office door opened and the receptionist stuck her head in.

"I was thinking of making some tea. Would you like a pot?"

"Yes, thank you." Skinner seemed burdened by the necessity to appear pleasant. Strand could feel him restraining himself, capping his surliness. She assumed the questions would be pro forma until the receptionist returned with the tea and departed. But they began immediately, asking about her relationship with Nelson. They hinted at speculation about the intimacy of the friendship. If they had been courting, the DSS was interested in how long before marriage might be expected, what the combined incomes and buying power would be.

"We're both homophile!" Strand did not believe they didn't know something as public as that. The Society no longer penalised queer citizens, but monitored them subtly, to satisfy conservative fears and more importantly to predict economic trends.

"Yes, of course, but that hasn't precluded bonding in some cases." Strand listened to the swing of their words in the air. Bonding occurred between all kinds of people for a variety of reasons but the Society expected formally posted bans before any co-mingling of households took place, so that census and tax records could be maintained.

The receptionist slipped in quietly as they continued talking and set the tea pot on a side table. As Strand watched the shape of their bodies and the auras surrounding each of them, she noticed that she could hear the receptionist listening to her. It was just as Lynx had said: an empath-- the receptionist--was taking everything in.

Strand stayed open, observing, not thinking. She could feel the receptionist's continued attention just outside the door while she answered most of the inquiries by rote.

"Have you considered that there might be more than friendship between you? At least on one side?"

Strand was flooded with deep surprise as she registered the question.

"No," she said hesitantly. "No, I really haven't. We spend time together. But..." her voice trailed off as she watched them seem to gather themselves, becoming taller, more authoritative.

"We noticed you both declared in the same religion on your tax returns." McKinnon's smile had too many sides.

Strand shrugged with amusement. You had to fill in a box so she'd filled in a box. She knew Nelson felt the same.

"We don't want to interfere, my dear," Skinner said. "But think about it. If he's bi-sexual you must take things into consideration. What signals you're giving..."

"Misunderstanding and miscommunication lead us to mistakes and misgivings," McKinnon broke in. Strand recognised McKinnon's quote from her own writing.

"As you know, our feelings lean toward more diverse unions. It's one way we help to break down barriers between groups and stablise our nation," McKinnon said with a smile.

"Of course, it's a very...strategic approach," Strand responded.

They smiled at her as if they shared a secret. She stared back diffusely. Her back felt irritated so she shifted forward in her chair during the long silence. Without looking at them directly she could sense them waiting, a blank wall of anticipation. But the receptionist outside was a magnet, drawing in Strand's unspoken thoughts and feelings. Strand remained equally open, almost providing a mirror.

Then McKinnon said, "And this trip to the farm, with our E Corp member?"

Strand took a deep breath. She'd prepared herself for any questions but hoped her voice didn't reveal her anxiety.

"Anything for my advertising clients, right?" Strand used her clipped, hard-edged tone making it sound like she barely remembered Lynx or the farm. "I met her at the art class. Then I begged the girl to let me visit on her next trip home so I get an updated sense of that stuff, you know: grass, cows, all that for when I go back in the simroom! Funny how the image of chickens needs a computer refine periodically, right?"

"Again, careful about how you express your affections."

"Affection? I'm sure that has nothing to do with my research," Strand said with a well-practiced, dismissive sniff. "But you've given me much to think about." Strand was happy she'd recently had her teeth whitened so she

46

levered her smile up to dazzle.

"Well now. We mustn't keep you from your work."

"I really appreciate this chance to meet you." McKinnon said. "Broadcast is so interesting. You've done some fine work. Didn't you do that potato chip advertisement?"

"No. But thank you."

"Thank you for being so candid, Burroughs." Skinner bent his lips into a thin smile.

Strand was soon back outside on the sidewalk. She didn't recall the descent in the elevator but she did remember saying good-bye to each of them, including Cynthia, the receptionist, whose name had slipped into her mind as she was listening. She remained in as open a state as she could all the way back to her office. Once there she rested her head on her desk. *Cynthia had been wearing a wig,* she thought, then slept exhausted for the better part of an hour.

SESSION #96

Nelson walked around his small parlour listening to Strand. He picked up a miniature of an Ashanti stool and let his fingers run tenderly along its curved wooden lines. He imagined a gold encrusted stool with an Ashanti king poised regally.

"You need to know they're suspicious."

"The Joneses are always suspicious."

"Nelson, don't. This could be your career, your life!"

47

"I get it, Strand."

"I don't want this to work for us and you end up with nothing."

"You know about my name, right?"

"It was your mother's last name?"

"No. It was my mother's first name. And her mother before that. Over a hundred years. For this political leader who got put in jail in what used to be South Africa."

"I know."

"Just about everybody gave up hope he'd ever get out. Except a few who kept on petitioning and kept the fight going. When he got out, the children he left behind, the partisans who were working for his freedom, they were all grown up. But they were still his children. They were different people, but they were, somewhere inside, still the same. That's what I think will happen when we're done."

Nelson sat the small carving down carefully on a shelf alongside a miniature of the recently demolished Arc de Triomphe.

"I want that moment when we look at each other and know, whatever the cost, we did something incredible, that nothing will ever be the same again. What is it you want from this, Strand?"

In the intensity of his voice Strand sensed Nelson weighing her. She chose her words carefully.

"I want to touch people," she said haltingly. "Not just seduce them into buying things or be gawked at when we go to premieres."

She took a breath to begin again. "I never allowed

anyone in when I was a kid. Too risky, you know. My mother was there one day and gone the next. I remembered her; did I ever tell you that? Not much: her smell, the way her shadow fell over me when I was in bed. Then she evaporated. Once dumped, twice shy." Strand almost laughed. "Then I met you and Lynx. Before that everyone was outside that glass, you know."

"There are easier ways to break down barriers."

"But with this it's not just me. We can keep Lynx out of a hospital. Her work can go on, maybe even better than before."

Nelson could see Strand's thoughts taking shape as she was speaking. She was clarifying motives for herself as well as for him.

"This is not like Faust, or some shit like that, Nelson."

"I love it when you do the classics," he laughed.

"I feel like I'm sweeping up broken glass." Urgency rang in her voice. "I've got to do it, I don't know what to do once it's up off the floor, but we've got to do it."

Nelson said nothing. Strand remembered her visit to the DSS.

"You know Skinner thought you and I might soon be posting bans!"

Laughter exploded from Nelson, the steeply angled light bouncing off the pristine shine of his head.

"I love your body, but I'm not that type of guy," he said through rippling giggles.

"And our colours match, so no go!" Strand said mischievously.

"All right, assume the position."

He handed her the glass of tranq.

"Please just be careful, pay attention."

"Lay down, girlfriend. I'm doing colour on front. Tell me about the trip to see the mother last week."

Strand recognised the worn contours of the table against her back. She stared at the ceiling, which was covered with a pale wash of colors, overlapping and delicately blended.

"Mae looks a lot like Lynx. Different hair, of course. But her body, her eyes especially. It made me wonder if she might be an empath too. Repressed empaths are pretty common, Lynx says."

She could tell from the hum of his machine that Nelson was too deep into the work to respond. Then her eyes closed. She thought not of the visit to Lynx's mother but of the first time she'd visited Lynx in a hospital facility where she worked.

#It seemed like fun when they'd decided to do it, but standing at the elevator, Strand only felt awkward and anxious. After growing up in an institution, she hated them no matter what their purpose. Waiting for the elevator, she knew why. There was a smell which made institutions alien, inhospitable to human life. The scent of decay, layered over with disinfectant and waste. The enforced crispness made all that was hidden more threatening. On the children's floor the atmosphere was only a bit more inviting than in the lobby. Strand had come because she could never picture what Lynx did and because Lynx wanted her to.

"We can sit together on my break in about half an

hour."

Strand nodded her head, curious what she'd be watching, still unnerved.

"You sit in here. The mirrored wall lets you see. Just sit still, no swinging your legs or getting up and down. Alright?"

"Why do you work with the patients so late at night?"

"I think I'm strongest then. And they're freer; the air is quieter around us. It just works better."

Strand sat in an office chair in the small, darkened room and watched Lynx, wearing the yellow jacket with the bright red E Corps insignia enter the room. She was followed by a nurse who wheeled a chair transporting a young Chinese boy with a small build. About 15, he talked non-stop, angry words escaping in spurts, aimed not at the nurse or Lynx, but at someone not there. His swearing and temper didn't seem to perturb Lynx at all. Once helped onto the table by the nurse, he lay still almost immediately. The nurse moved away, closer to the door. He was a tall, husky middle aged man with curly hair; he look Italian.

"Alfred, you know why we're here, don't you?"

"Yeah."

"You know I want to help you."

"Yeah."

"I would never hurt you."

"Yeah."

"Do you want to be able to talk to the people you see around you?"

The young man was silent. His narrow frame twitched

51

as if he were on a drug.

"Do you want to be able to talk to the people around you, like me and the nurse?"

"Yeah."

"Will you let me touch you?"

"Yeah."

"Will you let me touch the others you talk to?"

Again, he was silent, then, "Yeah."

Strand strained forward in her chair and watched Lynx lean into the boy, moving her hands slowly in the air across his body.

"You're really healthy, Alfred. Strong and smart."

Alfred was quiet as Lynx poised her hands in the air-- one over his chest, the other near his head. She closed her eyes and slid into a slow, arrhythmic rocking. She bent in as if pulled toward him, held there and then eased away. The air around them shimmered and in the corner of her eye Strand saw the nurse gripping the doorknob behind him.

A light glowed, a spectrum of colours hovering and drifting as if carried on a breeze; then intensified as Lynx spoke.

"You keep yourself safe by talking to them, don't you?" Although her voice sounded relaxed, Lynx's body was rigid.

"Yes."

The pale shades deepened, becoming solid in the air, vibrating feverishly. Strand's eyes widened in disbelief.

"Good. Next time I'll talk to them. OK?"

"Yes."

"Good." Lynx took a deep breath and Strand could see she was unsteady. The light receded, the colours evaporated. Lynx shook her hands out at her sides and brushed the boy lightly on his forehead with a quick sweeping motion as if she could rid him of his affliction with a flick of the wrist. The boy watched Lynx closely while the nurse took his pulse and blood pressure. He made notes then helped Alfred back into the chair.

"Thank you, Giancarlo," Lynx drew herself up straighter as he started to wheel Alfred out of the room. "I'll walk back with you."

They disappeared out of Strand's view and it was another five minutes before Lynx returned.

"I never saw anything like that in my life," Strand said, trying to make sense of it.

"Children's Hospital is the easy shift." Lynx shivered as if she were chilled before continuing. "Alfred and I've been working for 6 months. This was a real breakthrough."

"He didn't talk much, but those colours..."

"He never talks to me!" Lynx interrupted, her excitement rippling through her exhaustion. "For months he'll talk a blue streak to those people in his head. And all I ever get is 'yeah.' But tonight, he said 'yes.' I could feel it coming like a giant wave. He made a decision to say 'yes!'

As she spoke, tears welled up in Lynx's eyes. Watching her, Strand understood what her work could do for the patients and for Lynx.

"I've got juice and snacks in my little room here. I need to lie down for a bit, do you mind? I wasn't prepared for this."

Strand didn't respond but knew she wasn't prepared either. She followed Lynx to a small room which held a platform with mattress and blanket, refrigerator, lamp and writing ledge. Built into the wall was a monitor of some sort. When Lynx saw her notice it, she said, "I can plug in there if I feel overwhelmed. Stereo!" She swept the headsets from the pillow, hung her jacket on a hook and lay down.

Strand sat in the desk chair and watched Lynx's breathing slow, noticing the soft curve of her breasts under the pale green sweater she wore. In ten minutes, Lynx opened her eyes and her color was back. She smiled as if she'd had all the rest she'd ever need.

"I can't believe it! Alfred said 'yes.' You heard him!"

"He did."

"I can't wait to show the tape to the staff. I think the nurse, that's Giancarlo, he's been doing what I asked. Keeping up conversation with Alfred even when he doesn't answer. Giancarlo was about ready to cry."

"The nurse seemed scared to me."

"I think everybody is a little scared of E Corps. We work together as a team—E Corps and a med staff member. Giancarlo's kind of new but he's alright. He's really wanted to be able to help out Alfred."

"Even I could tell something big was happening. Just the 'yes,' I mean."

"Nelson won't believe it when I tell him."

"Nelson?"

"He came here. To see me work once."

"Really? He never mentioned it."

"Just one day after class, I think. He was curious. I happened to be working with Alfred."

Strand felt a twinge of jealousy; an unfamiliar feeling she couldn't unscramble.

"What happens now?"

"Giancarlo and I meet with the medical team tomorrow, present our report. If it works, well, we get to work with Alfred a little more frequently. And we can start work on two other patients with the same presentation. There's a little girl, ten years old, I think, who talks non-stop; she has to be sedated to sleep. But she hasn't said a word directly to anyone around her since she was two. We want to begin touching her as soon as possible."

The assurance Lynx felt in her own world filled Strand with desire and with a sense of dread. Something in her life was changing and she could not control it.

"I can't tell you how much I admire what you're doing." Even as she spoke the words Strand laughed at their formality. Lynx reached out for her hand.

"I want that from you. And more." Lynx's hand burned in Strand's. The connection was like a tunnel opening between them. Strand no longer thought of pulling away.

"Got to get back," Lynx met Strand's gaze.

"Yeah, I mean..."

They both laughed; then Strand's discomfort was ended when Lynx brushed her lips softly across Strand's cheek, then her mouth. "Much more," Lynx repeated in Strand's ear before she stepped back and grabbed her jacket.

Strand's eyes popped open and she was again looking at the soft colours of Nelson's ceiling.

"She's an amazing woman, Nelson."

"You betcha."

"I keep thinking there should be some other way to make her stronger, safer."

"I know the equation doesn't work out right. But look at her like the Jones' do. She's a commodity. Top shelf, but still a product that makes things run well. What do you think the Jones' would do to keep her in their store?"

Strand knew. She worked with people who sold products all day. The whole Society was one grand merchandising scheme. Society City and every town east of St. Louis was little more than a shopping mall. The health care Lynx gave was the property of the Society; maybe the one beneficial thing it provided. If she could make a better profit for Society in some other city, some other country, or lying in a hospital bed, she'd be sent there to do her duty.

Strand left Nelson eager to curl up in her own room to escape from these thoughts.

SESSION #112

The evening was cool as Lynx and Strand walked toward Nelson's flat holding hands, something they rarely did in public. A small bronze figure sat in the shrubbery just before his building.

"And who's this supposed to be?" Lynx asked, aware of the gaps in her education.

"It's a Rodin. Rodin in miniature is an oxymoron," Strand answered, "Claudel's better anyway." They both laughed. They didn't ring the bell but stood together looking around them at the lawn and the pieces of sculpture. Lynx held on more tightly to Strand.

"Are you alright?"

"I am. It's just every day I go to the Correctional Hospital and I don't know what to expect. I'll be happy when we...when we don't have to go to any of these places. Broadcast, the hospitals."

"Soon. Try to hang on."

"I know. It'll be a relief to do the work somewhere else maybe, without them holding my leash."

"We'll do it together."

They laughed again and rang the bell.

Upstairs, Nelson had chilled a bottle of ginger ale and opened his door waving the bottle with exuberance as if it were champagne. An old pop tune played and a jazzy harmonica wafted through the stereo speakers as Nelson settled Lynx and Strand in chairs with glasses. He sank down into a large pillow on the floor. They looked at each other silently for a moment.

"Ginger ale?" Nelson said after he spilled a bit on the floor, "For the ancestors."

"Perfect. I'm going to the hospital from here."

He poured generously for each of them then the silence returned. In the time Strand and Lynx had known each other, spending hours in Nelson's flat or at Ruby's, words had never been this difficult for them.

"I got the present you two brought back from the farm but Strand never told me how it went with your mother," Nelson said. The tiny replica of an old fashioned tractor sat on the book case; the deep grooves of its oversized wheels next to the delicate white walls of the bright yellow model of the antique car.

"It was good, I think. Mae was relieved to see me and she loved Strand."

"You're kidding?"

"Hey, I thought you were my friend."

"Strand, honey, you know I love you but I don't think you ever called yourself a mother's delight."

"She was crazy about Strand," Lynx protested. "If Mae could find a man like Strand she'd be remarried in a minute."

"You go a long way between singles clubs out there." Strand only fiddled with her glass.

"There's a lot of Partisan activity in that region these days, working roads, like that."

"Partisans?" Strand asked.

"A couple of them rebuilt a fence for Mae once and did some other stuff. Four women traveling together, kind of working their way around the countryside, doing chores for women who needed it, bartering for food."

"Partisans?" Strand repeated, unable to decipher the meaning of the waver in her voice and hating that she felt so much like Society wanted her to feel.

"Don't believe everything the Jones' tell you, Strand, I keep telling you that."

Strand didn't respond; she rarely accepted the Society's word on anything. She saw for herself, too closely, how their word was constructed, deconstructed, and twisted. They understood that if an idea—no matter how outlandish—was repeated enough times people took it for truth. She herself was frequently one of those polishing up the words, making them go down smoother with citizens. But if she totally rejected Society, what did she believe in instead? That was where she always stopped when she thought about it.

Partisans were the complete unknown. But did mystery mean dangerous? Did living on the margins make one a terrorist as Society preached repeatedly? Having Nelson in her life had given her the promise of something else, hovering nearby. Learning how to care with Lynx had drawn it even closer in. She understood she needed to settle into the idea of 'mysterious' more easily if this project was going to succeed.

"Partisans are all different kinds of people, Strand. Women who want to live away from men, men committed to end violence, greeners. They do their own work, their own way. Sometimes missions overlap."

"If we move out west, we'll be seeing Partisans, Strand," Lynx said cautiously.

"You'll be needing Partisans."

"Time for the fun part," Lynx said before Strand could respond. They all clinked their glasses together then, as Nelson reached up from the floor, they put down the glasses and held hands.

"Hey, this is a grand adventure, remember?" Strand

said.

"It's working, isn't it." There was no question in Lynx's voice.

"Yep. I can feel the differences."

"Let's make a toast then." Lynx picked up her glass. "To?"

"Art and magic?" Strand said.

"Art is magic." said Nelson.

"Art is magic." They touched the rims of their glasses together again and sipped quietly until Lynx rose to leave. Strand felt a rush of affection and of fear as Nelson embraced Lynx at the door. When this was done, she'd never see them together again. She might never see Nelson again at all. *Was escaping the Society really a possibility? Was it worth losing this camaraderie?*

After Lynx left, Strand and Nelson settled easily into their task.

"Did you ever notice that you rub your head just before you start working? Every time."

"Um hum." Nelson nodded.

"Up or down."

"Down, I'm going right to the collar and cuff edges."

"I signed out on sick leave this week."

"It's time. Tranq?"

"Just a little." She sipped from the glass Nelson pulled from his refrigerator.

"Good to go?"

"Good to go."

He clicked on the machine, not expecting much conversation tonight. Strand glanced at the wall nearest

Nelson's kitchen, which was broken by a wide pass-through and a counter with stools. Above the opening, tacked to the walls, was a series of drawings--she and Lynx alternating, each subtly different from the one before it. She closed her eyes, no longer needing to see the images; she remembered what Lynx had looked like when they'd first met and now, she knew almost every line of her body.

#Standing in the field which was part of her mother's small farm, Lynx spread her arms, mimicking the tree behind her. Strand had watched, fascinated by the difference being on the farm had made. Even on the drive west, before they'd been outside Society City for an hour, Lynx had started to look less burdened. Here in the field Lynx's skin was luminous, the furrow of anxiety had disappeared from her forehead and her laughter no longer had an edge of hysteria. Even Strand herself was different. She felt kindly toward the livestock, the grass, even toward the neighbours who occasionally lurked at the end of the long road leading up to the house, hoping for a glimpse of their own local E Corps oddity.

In the quiet of the field, her arms raised to the sky, Lynx looked to Strand much as she had in the childhood pictures Mae had shown her over dinner.

"Do it," Lynx said.

Strand mirrored Lynx, raising her arms to the sky, closing her eyes.

"Keep listening. Everything you could ever want is right here, all around us."

Strand took the air deeply into her lungs. Her body

wavered slightly, then she felt the caress and support of the light breeze. The leaves sounded like a river moving over head, insects swooped and darted. A pungent farm smell hung in the air, as did the soft sound of cows nearby. Lynx and Strand did not touch but stood adjacent, synchronous and harmonious, their bodies like similar outfits on hangers in a department store.

Energy tingled through the air around them. Rather than straining, Strand relaxed into the sensations and then a memory flooded her: Mae brushing her hair. The feel of Mae's hands on Strand's neck and head was comforting. The soft bristles of the brush sweeping across her scalp, pulling through long red curls, were firm and reassuring. Further back in the memory Strand sensed not only Mae's enjoyment but fear. Just as Lynx had described it.

Strand dropped her arms and opened her eyes. She thought she'd cry but no tears came. Lynx put her arms around her and spoke softly in her ear, "You can feel my past now, can't you. Like I feel yours."

Strand had no need to answer.

"Mae fought her fear, that's the courageous thing," Lynx said.

"They were all afraid. Society's still afraid."

"That's why they're so dangerous." Lynx's voice had the authority Strand had heard in the hospital and an edge of determination. Here among the trees Lynx was solid. She was an extraordinary but natural force in the world, not a commodity.

"There are other things I hope you never have to feel. But I don't know that I can stop it."

Strand watched sadness fill Lynx's eyes.

"At the Prison Hospital. They deem some prisoners incorrigible."

"Who deems?"

"Some committee or other--the Jones.' They keep reporting the crime rate is down. Everybody's happy. Nobody wants to know."

"Know what?"

"We...the E Corps...we touch them. When we're ordered to we go deep enough inside and extract; we can take back their feelings."

Strand was silent, trying to understand.

"We take back *all* of their feelings." Lynx's voice was strained down to almost a whisper. She could barely push the words out. "They can't hurt anyone, ever. They can't do anything. Soon, without the feelings, they die on their own."

Shame seeped into Lynx's voice. "Every time it feels like it's killing me too."

Strand pulled Lynx to her trying to quiet the trembling that rippled through her. The breeze turned chilly with the set of the sun; they shivered in each other's arms.

"You cold, girl?" Nelson drew Strand back to the present. "You got goose bumps."

"I am a little."

"I'll jack up the heat." He turned the control on the floorboard heater. "I'm about done for the day."

"Really?"

"You've been lying out here more than two hours!"

"I can't tell anything for sure anymore. Disoriented is beginning to be my middle name."

"Look good on a marquee."

"The other day, before I filed the papers for my sick leave, I sat in on a department meeting. Everybody was throwing out ideas for a new campaign, some new music group the Society's pushing--kind of English, kind of rock, a little social conscience thrown in. They're doing an international release. So, I suggested we use an underlay of footage of John Lennon. The room went silent like I'd just spit on the table."

Nelson kept his eyes on the work but he could tell the usually hard lines of her voice were soft. Her mouth quivered slightly as she told the story.

"The exec says 'The guy's been dead over a hundred years, Strand. Who's gonna relate to that?'

That wasn't really what topped me off. The damned producer, twenty-five years old. He's heard five rock and roll sides in his entire life. He says, 'Forget Lennon. Wasn't there something about him and God?' Can you believe that?"

"Cogs in a wheel have fuzzy memories."

"But can you believe it! He knows as much about images as a turnip. I didn't know what to do. I wanted to slap him on his head. I leaned over, looked him in the eye and said, "God who?" and walked out. I've never done that before. The Broadcast producer almost had a coronary behind me."

"Nothing's the same anymore, honey."

"Then, when I got to my desk...I cried!"

"Take it easy. Don't be trying to take on the whole world yet."

"Lynx keeps saying the same thing."

"Are you going there tonight?"

"Lynx says we're having a romantic dinner. Do you think that means vegan?"

"Nope, chocolate."

"Are we on for tomorrow?"

"Let's hold up for a day, okay? I want you to get some rest."

Nelson sprayed the newly worked on sections and watched Strand tentatively put on her clothes, as if all of her energy had been drained away by remembering Broadcast One.

"I'm gonna go crosstown with you."

"You don't have..."

"Nix. Let's go." Nelson opened the door and grabbed one of his several voluminous garments from a hook by the door. They walked side by side in the cool evening air crossing the grassy quadrangle passing several perfect replicas—Modigliani, Savage, Basquiat without noticing them. At the curb Nelson raised his arm when he heard a jitney behind them and the wrist chip attracted the automatic conveyance. When it stopped, they boarded and rode silently across town.

Nelson stood on the sidewalk waiting for Strand to let herself in and go up in the oversized industrial elevator. When he heard the final clang, he glanced up at the window. When he turned away, he noticed, out of the corner of his eye, an old pair of running shoes suspended by their knotted strings from the street lamp. He smiled, pulled his large cape around him and walked toward Ruby's.

Once upstairs Strand let herself into Lynx's flat and laughed with joy at Lynx's preparations. They knew they were taking a chance to openly meet at Lynx's home, but it would all soon be over. Champagne glasses gleamed on a low coffee table, alongside colorful Melmac plates and cloth napkins. In the refrigerator were several small dishes with pickles, pate, cheese and a couple of things Strand couldn't identify.

The dog, Sliver, followed her around hoping for a treat, while Dot watched from her perch on the top of the stove. Strand, suddenly exhausted, lay across Lynx's bed. Her mind whirled with pictures she couldn't shut out-- co-workers she'd said goodbye to casually as she went on leave; Lynx's mother, Mae; the short, Society-sanctioned road west they'd driven to get to the farm which was really the last outpost going west. Her head started to feel achy and she considered taking a pill when she noticed that Sliver and Dot were stretched out around her. She closed her eyes and sank back into the comforter. Sliver and Dot nuzzled against her, one on either side; and Strand's thoughts slid away into a pool and swirled around each other until they'd evaporated.

Strand opened her eyes an hour later to see Lynx standing at the foot of the bed, watching her. Sliver and Dot sat up, waiting for her attention.

"Are you hungry?" Lynx asked. "These animals sure are."

"I'm sorry, I should have thought to feed them when I came in. I was just so wiped out I had to lie down."

"How are you feeling now?"

"Like I'm getting over a migraine."

"You lay still, I'll feed them and come back and join you."

Strand lay back on the pillows, enjoying the sounds of domesticity from the other room. She listened to Lynx turn on the shower, then opened her eyes again to see her standing nude in the doorway, her damp hair wrapped tightly in a knot at the top of her head. The rounded angles of her hips and arms seemed a little firmer. Her normally tanned and freckled skin was pink from the heat of the shower.

"I feel better now." Strand's voice was both languorous and eager.

Lynx helped her out of her clothes and knelt above her on the bed, aware of the tenderness of Strand's skin.

"Not as good as we're going to feel," Lynx said before their lips met. Straddling Strand's body, Lynx grew more excited. Their mouths pressed together Lynx touched one of Strand's breasts. Lynx moved down the bed and licked at the lines and colours on Strand's belly, hip bones, thighs, knees. She nipped at the hairs that protected Strand's mound and then pushed her tongue inside. The taste was almost salty; musk filled Lynx's head. The thrill of desire that Lynx's tongue elicited rippled through not just Strand's body but through Lynx as well. She pushed relentlessly with her tongue, then she slipped first one finger then two into the warmth of Strand's body.

The rhythm between them soon took them both to the edge. The sound of their joy filled the room. They both understood this might be their final time.

They slept lightly and awakened in the predawn hours. They found each other's bodies again before sinking deeply into sleep.

They slept until the middle of the next afternoon. Strand called into her office to be certain no final details had been left undone. She already felt as if she'd been away for months instead of days. Her only regret was not saying a real goodbye to Freda. When Lynx went to the hospital in the evening, Strand sat looking out the window of the flat onto the street of warehouses.

Strand found it funny that Freda should come to mind so vividly now. Memories of tasks they'd done together filled most of Strand's evening as she now sat quietly with the cat and dog, wondering why it was her secretary and not her job she missed. She stretched out on the couch and she closed her eyes, when she started to drift off, she felt another presence. She lay still, listening, and realised she was sensing Lynx just as Lynx was listening to her.

Strand's breathing slowed and she sank into a state between sleeping and waking. She perceived Lynx's thoughts and activities at the hospital as if she were by her side. When Lynx went in with a patient, Strand could feel the lights in her head rather than see them as she had when she'd watched through the mirror when Lynx worked. Her body felt hot but not uncomfortable. When Lynx pulled back from touching the patient Strand felt the release and was tired as Lynx recovered in her resting room before seeing another patient.

When Lynx got home, she found Strand lying on the couch as she'd been all evening. Lynx fed Dot and Sliver, and sat in the kitchen listening as they ate. The Jones' had made certain that her living space in the building was psychically insulated with electronic waves; a warm quiet was layered around her flat and the building. The relaxation almost emanated from the walls. When the animals finished, they followed her into the living room. She led Strand into the bedroom and helped her undress. Dot and Sliver waited at the foot of the bed until the two women climbed under the comforter where they lay in each other's arms. The cat and dog inched into the spaces around Lynx and Strand on the bed, they then all slept dreaming each other's dreams.

SESSION #124

The next afternoon the sun was unable to pull itself from behind the clouds. The air in Lynx's rooms was mired in dampness but no rain fell. Strand paced the flat, confined and irritable. Lynx prepared for her final days at the hospital. She noted Strand's dour mood but didn't question it. She asked Strand to make tea for them. Sitting at the small kitchen table they held onto their cups as if they were life rafts.

"Did you say why you'll be out?"

"No." Lynx shook her head. "I alerted Giancarlo so he could make alternative treatment schedules. I didn't say anything really. Just smiled conspiratorially. I think he thinks I'm doing something juicily elicit. Even we're allowed that once in a while."

Lynx smiled at the thought and went through the list of all she'd accomplished.

"I've brought all my notes on patients up to date. I managed to get a consult with someone in E Corp for each of my patients so no one will be left without a professional who has an interest in their case. I've done no deep work in a while so no patient has to be really disrupted by a new link. Giancarlo has really come to understand the work, Strand. He'll make sure treatment is followed through."

"My job was so easy to leave. No consequences, no meaning, really," Strand's voice was deflated by exhaustion.

"It had meaning to you. The visuals, creating images."

"We'll see what that means in the long run. It seems petty compared to healing."

"Art is magic. All art," Lynx said. "If we lose that we're back where we started--carving out replicas. We're both working for a government that's a corporation. Crime, corporations, advertising. It's all the same." The edge in her voice was new, raw.

"Have I got a Partisan on my hands now?"

Lynx smiled as she stood to go to the hospital.

"What time is Nelson coming over?"

"Not 'til 7."

"Get some rest."

"I think I will."

"I hear Mount St. Helens is quite lovely this time of

year." Lynx tried to cheer Strand.

"Then perhaps we better see her."

Strand paced the flat after Lynx left, feeling restless and tired but unable to lie down. She decided to go out for a walk and found herself on the street of her own flat. She went in and looked around as if they were the rooms of a stranger. The walls were covered with framed images. Glossy magazines sat in stacks around the couch and on the dining table. The book case held a few more magazines and awards she'd won for advertising jobs. There were three heavy screener discs sitting in bronze bases. When twirled they each emitted a crisp photo and tinkling music as they came to rest, celebrating past campaigns she'd developed.

Strand packed them in crumpled paper and nestled each carefully in three shoeboxes beside the awards she'd received. She wrapped the boxes in plain paper from one of her pads of sketch paper and addressed each in elaborate script—for Freda, for Truong the elderly messenger and Buster who'd been her driver whenever they went on location. She wrote 'thanks' and drew ornate borders around their names, grabbed her set of favourite ink pens from a drawer and left. She raised her arm and a jitney locked on and pulled up beside her to take her toward Broadcast One as she had for the past 8 years. She left the packages with the night guard and boarded another jitney to Ruby's. As she neared the familiar and brightly lit window, Strand felt a rush of warmth at its familiarity.

Once inside Strand wasn't sure it had been a good

idea. The cafe was bursting with people. Dishes, glasses and voices clattered in her head. Ruby waved her over.

"Sit at the bar with me," she said, recognising Strand's distress. She poured a glass of wine and watched as Strand took a sip.

"You don't look like you should be wandering around alone, my friend."

"I guess not. I'm not feeling so well."

"Danny," Ruby called behind her. A muscular, dark-skinned man with mixed gray hair appeared in the swinging doors. He looked somewhat familiar to Strand but with her mind in such a muddle she only managed to look puzzled.

"Will you give Nelson's friend a lift?" Ruby asked.

"Sure. Be right back." He disappeared back into the kitchen.

Ruby then turned to Strand, "Yeah, you met Danny before he transitioned. Remember, she was Donna then, maybe your first visit here?"

"Of course, I'm sorry...I..."

"Good lookin' ain't he!"

Strand smiled and nodded at the realisation that finding one's true self was a joy no matter the path.

"Thanks for the loan," Strand said.

Five minutes later Danny reappeared wearing a cap and sweater. He took Strand's arm as if he'd done it countless times before.

"Okay madam, we'll have you comfortable in no time."

His gravelly voice was soothing; its low pitch lulled

72

Strand easily. She remembered little of the ride back to Lynx's flat. She didn't even remember telling Danny where to take her. He parked and walked her to the door.

"Tell Nelson I said hey," Danny called over his shoulder as he casually turned back to his car as if he brought her home every night.

Strand lay down on the bed with Sliver and Dot at her sides until she heard Nelson ringing the doorbell.

He lugged his massage table inside and set a large bag on the floor.

"You look like you haven't slept since I was here last!"

"I think that's about all I've been doing." Strand hated the whine creeping into her voice.

"Well, sister love, this is gonna be it."

"You think?"

"It better be. DSS was at my house yesterday." He tried to sound casual but Strand heard the anger. She was surprised she heard no fear; a knot formed in her stomach.

"Don't worry, I've been keeping the machines in another spot ever since they called you in."

"If they confiscated your wonderful old machines, the Rogers, the Cindy Ray..."

"It's OK, they're safe." Nelson set the table up in the middle of the living room. "I've been prepared for this."

"What'll happen when we're gone?"

"Make the stereotypes work, honey. I'll be a public nuisance, grief and abandonment dressed in feathers and red; the hysterical victim of a calculating advertising bitch. Then drop into the background. Everybody will be so happy that the big, black queen shut up, things should

73

quiet down."

Anxiety kept Strand silent.

"I'm not leaving town," Nelson said to Strand's unasked question. "That would put DSS on me like a tracking bug." Dot rubbed against Nelson's leg and then against the table.

"Find a seat, puss," Nelson said firmly as he pulled a premixed bottle of tranquilliser from his bag. Dot crossed the room and sat on the back of the couch.

"You've got the touch," Strand said, "With the cat, I mean."

Nelson nodded and beckoned her to the table.

"This is going to be in your face." Nelson laughed. "It's mostly shading, no fine lines. But you need to really concentrate. And relax at the same time. I really mean relax. I have got options if something–untoward– happens here. Then you'd soon see me on your doorstep, if they have such things in the wild, before you can say silk and satin."

"Should we...I wondered...what..." Strand wasn't certain what question to ask.

"We'll just proceed like we always do. I'll work on your face and neck for a couple of hours, if you can. Then come back later and do your hands."

"I thought we were going to do it all at once."

"We'll see. The face work is more shadowing than anything else, but that's delicate. The hands are detail, we'll see."

"Can..." Strand started.

"Quaff!" Nelson handed Strand the bottle.

Strand took a sip and grimaced, "What is this—a double dose?!"

Nelson didn't answer as he set out inks. Strand put her clothes across the arm of the sofa and lay on the table.

"Up I assume."

"Yep," Nelson said and clicked on the machine, enjoying the delicately balanced weight in his hand.

"It's going to be fine, Strand. Just open up, let things in."

"Look who you're talking to."

"I am looking." With his other hand he brushed the softness of Strand's face. Her lips curved in a smile under his hand. Through the tips of his fingers, he felt her surrendering to the tranq.

"It's odd working here. Everything is right and wrong at the same time."

"Shhh."

Strand's body softened against the table, the hypnotic buzz of the machine filling her head as Nelson leaned toward her face. The vibrating of the needle was a large and frightening sound for a moment, then Strand was in darkness and the sound was her only reference point. She clung to it briefly then let it go, making room for memory of a moment that had been critical to their taking the path they were on.

#She'd waited outside the hospital for an hour before going up to see what was taking Lynx so long. Remembering the way from her visit several weeks earlier, she made her way up to the Children's floor. She couldn't decide what to say, what approach to take, so decided to do what she always did: act like she knew her way. That would conceal her fear that something had happened to Lynx.

As she got off the elevator, she found her way back to Lynx's resting room and opened the door quietly. It was empty. She walked in and opened the refrigerator. Bottles of water stood neatly alongside an unopened packet of cheese. Strand stepped back into the hall and closed the door.

She looked around, trying to blank out her uneasiness at being in the hospital, at not finding Lynx. She'd decided to talk to the floor nurse back near the elevator when she saw Lynx's nurse/partner coming toward her and was relieved she remembered his name.

"Hello, Giancarlo, my name is Strand. I don't know if..."

"Oh, sure..." The smile of recognition faded and the angle of his body and his silence told Strand something was wrong.

"I'm looking for Lynx. She was due to get off over an hour ago."

"She had to leave." Giancarlo looked as uncomfortable as he had the night Strand had watched him through the mirror while Lynx worked on the young patient.

"What does that mean?"

"They...I mean she was ill. We were working with one of the children. And she slipped."

"She fell?" Strand felt overwhelmed by information she couldn't decipher. The place, his words all seemed a jumble.

"No. Come inside, that'd be better." She and Giancarlo stepped back into Lynx's resting room. They were the same height but his bulk made the room and Strand feel small. He leaned back against the door in the same way he had when she'd first seen him: holding onto the doorknob behind his back.

"She slipped...off centre...I guess is the best way to explain it. I don't know how much you know..."

"Just tell me what happened, I'll figure it out."

"She slipped off centre. Her touch was not simply reaching inside the patient; she was losing herself. She insisted on finishing with this one patient. She's been working a lot, too much really, in the last couple of months. She just wanted to finish up so the kid could go on to the next phase of treatment."

"But what happened, exactly?"

"I took the girl back to her room, and when I didn't see Lynx, I came back to the treatment room and she was standing but completely unfocussed. Like she was unconscious, but standing." Giancarlo's voice shook with emotion. Strand could see why Lynx had such faith in him.

"I know the procedure so I just eased her onto a gurney, strapped her down and covered her with a blanket."

"Strapped her down!" Strand couldn't keep outrage out of her voice.

"So, she wouldn't fall out. That's the procedure." Giancarlo's tone asked Strand to understand. "Then I called the E Corps officer. We're not supposed to touch any member of the E Corps. I took her pulse, though. I had to...to see what I could. It was very slow, slower than anything I'd ever felt. But she was in there, I could tell. Then they came."

"Where'd they take her?"

"I don't know. This has only happened twice the whole time I've been here. Both times they brought them back to their resting rooms, but they bundled Lynx into a van. They wouldn't even talk to me. Just made me tell them everything that had happened in the session with the kid. And afterwards. I'd already started writing my chart notes. They took them away! Can you believe that shit? I've got to write them out all over again for the kid's file!"

"They took your notes?"

"They flew out of here like they were going to a fire. But I tell you she's going to be fine. I'm sure of it. She was already pulling it back together, she just needed time. I don't know why they..."

Strand turned abruptly toward the elevator. She turned back quickly, "Thanks, Giancarlo. I'm sure you're right. I'll just go by her flat. Thank you."

Strand rushed back to Lynx's, not expecting to find her there but still disappointed that she didn't. She sat heavily on the sofa, about to call Nelson when she realised the cat and dog were watching her. She almost rose to feed them then noted how intently they were staring. It was different from their customary food longing-filled gaze. They sat side by side across the room, their pupils slightly dilated.

She decided to do what Lynx was always suggesting--

she listened. She opened up her awareness and heard the room, the space around her. She gazed at Sliver and Dot, who were sitting more still than she'd ever seen them. Nothing interrupted their attention. Then she heard Lynx, a slow surfacing of thoughts inside Strand's head as if they were her own.

"I'll be fine. There's only one way. Steady. Close down. Shut out all. Drugs run their course. Close down. I'll be fine."

Strand sat on the couch as if paralysed. The thoughts were coming to her from Lynx, she was certain. But she didn't know what to do. Tears started to roll down her cheeks and she touched them, puzzled.

She woke in the middle of the night, her head resting on the back of the couch and a dull headache clouding her memory. Sliver and Dot were still sitting side by side, but facing the door. A few moments later it opened and Lynx came in. She seemed so deflated Strand almost didn't recognise her in the dark.

"What does it mean?" she asked Lynx.

"I had a hard time holding on to my focus. The closer we become the more difficult it is for me."

"Why?"

"I can't explain it. Think about yourself, Strand." Lynx's voice was weak but had an undercurrent of urgency. "You keep yourself under tight control most of the time. You haven't given a thought to anything but work, the machinations of Broadcast One, for almost 10 years. No real life, or friends, except Nelson. And he takes you exactly as you are, without making demands. You don't do any charity work, don't go through drama with friends, don't sympathise with anything."

Strand's head was pounding but she could hear Lynx's words were not said in anger but sadness.

"Sit, let me," Lynx said and waited for Strand to sit back on the couch.

"You're a wonderful woman, Strand." Lynx held her hands close to Strand's forehead. "But it's buried very deep inside. You've got armour on your armour. That's why it scared you to know how much I cared for you. Then you had to open up to me. And once you really do, all kinds of things can happen. And that scares you. If you're not the Strand you used to be, who are you?"

"Things are better."

"No, I'm losing strength, Strand. Every night at the hospital I'm less focused. And they notice."

Strand was chilled to the core. She grabbed Lynx's hand which almost glowed with heat. "I won't let them take you away!"

The next evening Lynx did not work and they arranged to meet Nelson for dinner at Ruby's. The answer came to them there as they listened to him talking about a tattoo he'd done 10 years before: the heart of a lion on the breast of a young woman.

"I logged onto a med library. Finding full-colour zoological pictures of internal organs is no easy slide, let me tell you." Enthusiasm was fresh in Nelson's voice. "It was perfect--aorta, ventricles, veins--full colour. And she needed it, you know. She was just at a place where she could leave some garbage behind; this was the push she needed. A couple months later, when she came by my place to say thanks, I could see the difference before she said a word. She was filling out her...herself, like she wasn't even there before. I been tattooing ever since."

Strand and Lynx both glowed with a frisson of understanding. The tattoo was more than the symbol: it was the essence. Through their mutual weaknesses they could create strength.

"Strand. Strand?" Nelson's voice was distant and slow as if he were talking through mud. When she opened her eyes the light's glare forced her to close them again quickly.

"Sorry," Nelson moved forward to block the light. "You were a little too still for my tastes, girlfriend."

"I was remembering that night at Ruby's when you told us about the lion heart tattoo." She squinted to see the outline of Nelson's shining head.

"You two the ones with heart." He clicked off the light. "Okay. You're really doing great. I'm gonna hold up here for now. I'm not spraying your face. You ain't going nowhere, are you?" He laughed as he said it.

After helping Strand up, he folded his table and put it in the corner, cleaned his instruments, wrapped them in cloth and slid them into the deep pockets of his long coat.

"What time will Lynx be home?"

Strand looked at her watch, "Not 'til much later, she's going on break about now."

"Don't touch anything. Let Lynx work on you when she gets in. Just a little. Not too much."

"Yes sir."

"Wish I could have that answer on tape. Tomorrow, the hands, seven pm. This is working, Strand, we don't know exactly what that means but just stay steady, hear me?"

"I'm a rock...at least at this moment."

After Nelson left Strand lay on the bed, Sliver and Dot beside her, but she didn't fall asleep until just before Lynx came in. She moved quietly through the rooms, taking a shower, feeding the animals before she came to the bedside. Holding her hands over Strand's face she moved slowly, letting the heat build then releasing the energy. Strand lay still without speaking.

"I can almost see it." Lynx said. "But don't look until later."

"I don't need to look. I can feel it, inside. He finishes tomorrow he thinks. The hands."

"I know." Lynx took Strand's hands in hers and kissed each finger. She rolled her tongue around them, sucking, tasting, enjoying the way they pressed against the inside of her mouth. The evening in Ruby's seemed very long ago to both of them.

Lynx pressed Strand's hands to her breast until their heart beats returned to normal. Then they lay side by side until the next afternoon.

SESSION #146

Nelson set up the table and puttered around the room,

not sure what he wanted to do, uncertain in a place not his own.

"I'm not worried," Strand said. "Not anymore."

"I didn't think so. Maybe I'm the one who's worried. You'll be on the move, out west. I'll have to come out to the boondocks to visit. Ugh!" He shivered in exaggerated distaste.

"Perhaps you know some handsome Partisans you'll be wanting to visit."

"Mebbe, as my great grandfather used to say."

They both looked around the room, knowing it would be the last time they saw it in quite this way.

"I'm going to have you lay down as usual, since that's how we're used to working. But I'm going to stretch out your arm to the dining table, OK?" He spread towels on the table as he spoke. Strand sipped at the bottle of tranq, then climbed on to the table with a familiarity she was sure she'd miss.

"Nelson."

He looked up from the ink he was mixing.

"I don't know what to say, I guess."

He strapped the needle machine to his hand. "You'll get a package in a couple of days with information you'll need once you're out of the city. Lynx's mother's farm will be the confirmation point so I'll know you've made it that far. Toss the shoes but don't tarry there. Just keep going west 'til you decide to settle down. Partisans will help."

"Sounds so simple."

"It is and it isn't. And I'll want a postcard."

"I know, I know. It's not just about not having people

on the card, is it? It's the possibilities. Open space, not corrupted, no one trying to sell you something.

"Sounds good to me."

"Then you better come out west."

"And who'll help out the folks back here?"

Strand relaxed, feeling the animals watching from the other side of the room. The machine clicked on.

"You know I've only been mad at you once, all the time we've been friends?"

"Um hum. No talking now though." Nelson leaned forward and the glare of his light washed over her arm. Strand closed her eyes, remembering the second time Lynx had been hospitalised.

#She'd waited at home for several hours, expecting Lynx to call. She tried the hospital, then Lynx's home. Then she decided to sit and listen as she'd done before but nothing came through. Since they'd been working on the tattoo they were entwined, inseparable, even when they were on opposite ends of town. Each had become a soft hum in the other's mind, a slight vibration under each other's skin.

Strand didn't understand what was happening. She leapt up from the couch and slammed out of her flat, running toward Nelson's. When she rang the bell, she realised it was late, but he buzzed her in without asking who it was.

As she walked in, before she could speak, he said, "I know. She'll be alright."

Something in his voice stopped Strand.

"How can you know that?"

"She should have stopped working earlier. Things are too fragile right now."

"How can you know any of this?"

"Sit down. I'm sorry we didn't talk about this possibility. She just had an episode."

"She slipped." Strand did not sit down.

"Yes, she slipped. Not good but not totally uncommon. She should not have been doing such deep work while all this is going on."

Strand's eyes narrowed as she looked at her friend. She was increasingly uneasy and not sure why his words weren't comforting. She repeated her question.

"You know, don't you? Just like Sliver and Dot know."

Strand stalked across the room which looked odd without the massage table sitting at its core. She turned at the kitchen and looked again at Nelson. "You're one too!"

His eyes and hands were unnaturally still, Strand noticed.

"You're an empath too!" Strand almost screamed. "Why were you hiding it—from me?" Strand twisted around as if looking for something to break then collapsed against a stool at the counter.

"I've hid it all my life, Strand. I never wanted to be forced to fight the Society to have a life. Whatever healing I do I do on my own."

"You've been my friend for how long?" Strand moved in closer. "We've been working on this project for over a year. You couldn't tell me?"

"You won't know what it's like to be owned by the State until we're finished with this project. Even then it'll be a memory, not the life you live every day. Lynx knows. And I saw it happen to my best friend when I was 14." Nelson pulled his caftan around him protectively and looked at his shelves filled with its tiny toys. "We planned to visit all those places that don't exist anymore. Old tourist spots. We figured the vibes would be wondrous. We were inseparable. Finished each other's sentences. Wore each other's clothes. Knew how to comfort each other. I loved him.

"They took him away when they found out. After that he made one visit back to see his parents—he hardly spoke to them. Or to me, when I showed up. I could feel him struggling to make sense of us; so many other voices and lives were inside him. It was like we were all ghosts in some former life he'd had. Then he split for good."

"It wasn't until he was gone for almost a year that I figured it out. It wasn't just him. It was me, too. Without me, he almost couldn't handle it. I shaved my head so no one would know. And I stay repressed so other empaths can't find me."

"Why couldn't you tell me, once we started working?" Strand could feel the tears of betrayal welling up inside her.

"To explain in words ain't that easy, Strand. I know that's part of what we're supposed to do, that's why they gave us the education, the training. But sometimes words just don't explain anything."

"Does Lynx...of course she knows. Doesn't she?"

"When she walked into the class it was like I was knocked off my feet by a gale force wind. I'd kept everything clamped down, except when I did tattooing. Then I tried to help people, kind of like Lynx does at the hospital. But by the second session she was speaking to me in my head. We both knew we were going to do something wonderful. We weren't sure what, but then you kept asking about her. And she wanted to meet you."

"You two planned this!"

"No. We never planned anything. We felt our way to it. Untangled the mass of confusion and connections and here we are."

Anger nudged against Strand until she kicked it away. They hadn't tricked her; everything there was to know they'd revealed.

When you're not blocking us out you hear.

Strand heard Nelson's voice in her head. The round tones she'd listened to for hours calmed her now.

"It's really going to work, isn't it?"

"It is working. You both made the choice, Strand. A good choice."

"It's like you're someone else I don't know."

"No, it's just that now you know me better. As my great grandfather used to say, 'What real queen shows all his cards at once?'"

"Your great grandfather knew more than any great grandfather I ever heard of."

"He was queer too! Didn't I ever tell you that story?"

Strand opened her eyes as Nelson sprayed fixative

87

on her hands. The lines of shading on her forearms and the backs of her hands were subtle even before healing. Nelson watched her face. Her approval pleased him.

"I don't know how much better it could be. I feel like I'm always telling you to relax. But a major ingredient in healing is rest."

"Nelson...I love you," Strand squeezed the words out of her heart knowing she needed to say them as much as he deserved to hear them.

"I knew you could do it. Now let me have one final look."

Strand stepped out of her tunic and pants as Nelson turned the light onto her full body. She stood as naked and still as Lynx had done in their class as Nelson circled her, looking at the lines he'd drawn, the colours he'd added.

Each joint, fold, wrinkle delicately matched. Lines and perspectives balanced; inks blended. Strand stood as if she were a grand Māori woman warrior, the worlds inside of her mirrored by the fleshly lines. Nelson had never done such an extensive tattoo and was amazed himself by the impact. As he watched the lines shifted and flowed with a life separate from Strand.

"What about the wheels?" Strand said, alarmed as she remembered the bicycle tattoo on her calf.

"Not to worry. We've got it."

Strand decided she was done asking questions. Nelson walked around her one last time then said, "See you on the trail, sister."

"Not before we leave?"

"No." He pulled the table out into the hall then kissed

her head.

"I feel like we should say something more."

"We're not saying goodbye."

"In the orphanage, all those people I grew up with--the kids, the counsellors--they came and went like lights blinking on and off. They're a blur to me. Even the people I worked with every day at Broadcast, I could barely remember them or their lives when I wasn't in the office. That won't be true with you, Nelson."

"We do get to pick our people, Strand; and we picked well." He held his hand in front of her face, almost caressing her cheek. Heat flowed between her healing skin and his palm. He closed his hand and a cool breeze drifted in as he picked up his bag.

Strand listened to the elevator descending, clanging and squealing as usual. But nothing felt usual. Once Nelson was gone Strand was listless. She'd always been proud that she was going into middle age in good condition. But the past few months had worn her down in ways

she couldn't account for. She was determined to not be in bed when Lynx came home this last time; so sat at the dining table and read a real book. She found one on the kitchen shelf and turned the pages gingerly.

Lynx came in earlier than previous nights and found Strand asleep with her head down on the table, the book her pillow.

After taking her shower she stood over Strand, admiring the work Nelson had done on her hands. She held her own out beside them and her breath caught. She woke Strand gently.

"I have to show you something."

"Ooh. I'm sorry I fell asleep."

"It's late, of course you're asleep. We'll both be soon. But look." Lynx pivoted on her foot to display her calf. On it was a fresh tattoo--a penny-farthing which matched Strand's. The large, spoked wheel, delicately connected to the smaller wheel behind, curved with the muscles in her leg.

"When'd he do that?" Strand said excited. "How'd he do that?"

"Tonight. It was alright! I was fine the whole time!"

Strand was amazed that Lynx could bare the needles long enough for a tattoo even this simple.

"Let's go to bed." Lynx nudged Strand from behind. Her long red and silver hair, still wet from the shower, left a string of droplets across the floor which Dot pounced on.

They lay in bed in silence until Dot and Sliver jumped up on either side of them. They all dropped off to sleep. Just before dawn Strand woke for a moment but Lynx was not in the bed. She tried to hear her in the other rooms but it was silent. Before she could call out, she was asleep again. They both slept through the next day. In the late afternoon Strand got up to close the curtains against the sunlight.

"Are you hungry?" she asked Lynx, who watched her from the bed.

"No. I..."

"I'll feed Dot and Sliver." Strand started to leave then

sensed something. "What is it?" Strand couldn't conceal the alarm in her voice.

"I can't move...I don't think."

In one leap Strand was kneeling beside the bed. "What...?" Her voice was strangled with fear. Lynx lay on her back, arms limp by her sides.

"It'll be okay." Lynx's breathing was shallow. "I just... remember those old television shows we saw once. They used to take people's molecules apart to transport them somewhere then put them back together? Remember how we laughed?"

Strand only nodded.

"My skin is prickly, like needles all over. It feels like my molecules are moving. Away from each other."

Strand sucked in her breath trying to decide what to do.

"Nothing. Let me lie still and see what happens. Go do the food."

Strand reluctantly went out to the kitchen to feed the animals. By the time she returned Lynx's entropy was dispelled, she'd curled into a ball and was sleeping. Strand crawled in, curled around her and they slept again into the night. Dot and Sliver didn't join them.

Sometime after midnight Lynx awoke, relieved to feel her limbs returned to normal. She got up to look out the window. She pulled the curtains back and let the street light shine in, smiling at the pair of shoes hanging from it. Nelson had told her to look for that sign wherever they went. Lynx turned back to the bed where a shaft of light from the window spilled over Strand. The new lines on Strand's face were already healed. It was amazing yet natural to Lynx. Strand shifted under the sheet, restless but deeply asleep; as she turned Lynx started in shock. Strand's arm, which lay on top of the sheet, was almost transparent. The wrinkle of the bedding underneath was outlined almost perfectly–through Strand's arm.

Terror flooded through Lynx's chest. She snapped the curtain shut and continued to watch Strand, now barely visible in the dark, and took long, slow breaths until her pulse returned to normal. After a few minutes she realised she was too groggy to stand any longer. Lynx returned to bed, slipped gingerly under the sheet. She lay on her back letting the calf of her leg with its new penny farthing tattoo lightly touch Strand's twin tattoo. She thought she heard a mild whirring sound but was asleep before she could reach out to touch Strand. As she fell more deeply into sleep their dreams overlapped.

Light lifted from their bodies and swirled around as if on a giant disc. Their light, all the shades of it, spiraled until they blurred. Lynx turned and rustled in the sheets. Strand lay still, her body sapped of strength. Through the night the spiraling and spinning swelled in their dream until it was a sound of wheels turning, filling their heads. The whirring grew, engulfing the room, spinning with colours. Now the light that rose from their bodies formed an arc above them which was drawn into dancing hues. Lynx turned onto her back, Strand onto her stomach, then reversed. And they dreamed the turning until just before dawn.

They lay facing each other. Lynx opened her eyes first,

then Strand. Lynx stretched and rolled onto her back, opening her arms; Strand slipped into her embrace this one last time. With eyes closed they explored each other—hands, mouth, skin—each savouring the feeling of flesh on flesh until they could feel it no longer. The sensations of two became one.

When the sun was full in the sky, beating hard on the closed curtains, Dot and Sliver jumped onto the bed and settled themselves around a sleeping woman.

II. TRYNA

Earlier she'd opened her eyes twice, stared toward the ceiling and experienced a complete lack of memory. This time when she awoke, she knew a name to be hers—Tryna. That her memory wasn't any broader sparked a small flame of panic. But, on its own, her body remembered enough to catapult from the bed, muscles taut with the knowledge she had to escape. Nelson—his name formed in her mind—seemed to have settled on all the necessities: she saw a backpack standing at attention by the door. She scanned the room seeing it for the first and the last time; then picked up a photograph from the dresser which showed Nelson, rotund, brown, and smiling. His face triggered the information he'd planted in her mind. In the picture he was embraced by two women she recognized. One was Lynx: short, compact, white skin arrayed with freckles and a shock of silver cutting through her long orange hair. The other woman, Strand, was dark-skinned, tight lipped; her maze of braids was dyed blue. Tryna slipped the snapshot out of its frame and into a plastic folder in the pack.

The dog, Sliver and cat, Dot sat still. Realizing she knew them too damped down her fear a little more. Accustomed to listening and acting in concert with her, or at least with part of her, they watched closely. She touched them tentatively then went to the bathroom mirror. She turned the light up high gazing at herself for the first time: tall, coppery complexion, deeper copper freckles, eyes an almost translucent brown and a flood of silvery hair. Her skin felt like thousands of tiny moths were giggling and fluttering around just under the surface.

Whispering voices inside her head made her squeeze her eyes shut as if she could conjure up silence. But when she opened them, the slight sense of movement beneath her skin made her gorge well up. She fought down the nausea but bent over the commode. She knew it was them wanting to remind her why they all were there. No vomit but she did need to pee. When she was done, she turned on the water in the sink but pulled her hand back in terror. Suddenly it seemed the water might wash her away. Her hands glowed slightly has she turned them in the glare of the bathroom mirror light. She understood then that this was the moment of her death and her birth.

Nelson, Lynx and Strand had expected magic but none of them had been prepared for this. This tattoo was not like the ephemera approved by Society. Nelson had known there was power in his hands but not its extent. Inking the image of one woman, Lynx onto the body of her lover, Strand, had been designed to unite their spirits, bonding the two, making a stronger whole—for the two of them. They each knew any outcome was better than a muted death for Lynx. At least they'd hoped so.

When Tryna, this third being, emerged from their union Nelson was stunned and frightened, but there was no reversal of his magic. As they'd slept, he'd slipped in and stared down at this new being and returned with the papers and information they would need. Now Lynx and Strand stared into the mirror through Tryna's eyes. Both inside of her—one Black one white; one empath the other walled off from her feelings—Tryna wondered what that made her? At that thought Tryna's head filled with the clamor of two very different voices eager to debate her questions. Benevolence was about to turn into bad news.

What you feel will guide you.
Reality is what's visible, follow that!
You must feel before you can see anything.
Society doesn't reward feelings, believe me!

"Can we agree to hold the noise down for a bit while I try to get us out of here and on the road without people noticing?" Tryna said softly.

The voices inside went silent. She remembered Nelson calling them two lovers who foment change.

"You'll take their skills and join the ones in the west who do not accept falsehoods, who do not look for gods to soothe or save them. You'll use the powers of three women now," he'd said, while she slept, like a teacher imparting a final lesson. Nelson's magic and his art had cheated Society out of two of its most precious commodities, so it was time to run.

"His instructions say we go north to the Mamaroneck crossing then find the bikeways which we take west to Mae's farm. We have to avoid the primary road." Tryna felt a small leap in her heart...in Lynx's heart, at the mention of her mother.

"I don't know about this mother thing. I don't know what Mae will say or feel when we present ourselves but

Nelson was clear: we have to visit her farm before we push on toward the Great Sunders, okay? Please don't answer!" Tryna demanded, as if wrangling unruly school children.

She returned to the backpack with supplies, new 'official' papers, food; when she dug deeper, she found a miniature of the Eiffel Tower. Tears sprang to Tryna's eyes as Lynx remembered how much Nelson treasured his collection of miniature landmarks, the originals of which had mostly been demolished in the previous century. First bombs, then convoluted government decrees around the world had leveled most outstanding architecture in an effort to create a uniform Society without extremes, they'd said, which engender envy and rivalries.

She pulled out a folder marked mysteriously "AAA." She found inside a series of paper maps and instructions about protecting herself on the road. It also included a pamphlet describing the different communities she'd find beyond the Sunder, the activities of the Partisans and assorted skills that were needed to rebuild a new society in the free west. She returned the folder to the pack. It also contained the promise of Partisans and Dreamers who would both help and need her. Beside the pack sat a wheeled travois, to transport the cat and dog. It would be disaster to be seen traveling with animals given the Society's distaste for keeping pets. The only conclusion would be that she was an empath and that attention could be fatal.

Along with Nelson's escape instructions, the information held by both Lynx and Strand was a wealth of knowledge if Tryna could navigate it through the chatty two voices competing within for her attention.

You cannot carry electronic devises with you!

Let's be sure to...

"Nelson already said that in his instructions." Tryna said impatiently as she opened a window, waited for an open top truck to pass then tossed her communicators down into its depth as it sped south. The electronic screen she unplugged and left sitting dark like an eye closed forever. She painted her face with geometric figures to confound street cameras and grabbed the umbrella Nelson had constructed especially for her. It was able to bounce back and scramble eye-in-the-sky signals.

In the late evening she loaded her pack onto her back with its animal-heavy travois attached, stepped into the street and walked briskly to the edge of Society City, the heart of the Eastern US government. Tryna's stride was long and strong as she turned north along the railroad tracks. Suburban communities had once oozed north from the city until homegrown militia had terrorized any one deemed unacceptable. Their violence was amplified by criminal gangs peddling narcotics which hollowed out the population.

When the multiple viral infections proliferated citizens rebelled against safeguards the population numbers continued to drop until the civic infrastructure was meaningless. Finally, the careerism of elected officials conflated with corporate greed created a perfect vacuum. Wealthy political action groups recalled office holders who didn't agree with them then they amplified local police with the military.

People didn't remember when authorities gave up fighting the root of the problem but few had the resources or the energy or most importantly, the trust to sustain life very far away from the city centers. Simultaneously, as the population decreased precipitously from contagion, poverty, crime fatalities as well as fallout from the toxins infiltrating the ground water and air spelled the end of society as it had been known. It had happened so slowly few recognized the link between falling birth rates and ecological disaster. Many politicians had sworn that God wouldn't let such things happen and too many people listened as if they didn't know better.

Then the earthquakes of 2060 had split the US in thirds. After years of concern about the San Andreas Fault on the west coast the surprise came from unexpected geological plate shifts along the New Madrid Fault traversing the Midwest and South. Then more devastating was the Ramapo Fault rift, closer to the east coast, which destroyed a nuclear power plant located just on its line. The fall out had killed thousands and poisoned the groundwater for miles around.

Other countries suffered some geophysical catastrophes as well, as if the earth itself wanted to punish humans for acting like warring children. However, the split between east, central and west in the United States was so dramatic the eastern states actively cut connections with the lands that lie beyond what came to be known as the Great Sunders. A new corporatized government emerged, the Society, which decreed the states were more a loose association than a nation, and impeded travel beyond the Ramapo Sunder for fear of losing more of its population.

This socio/geological history floated in Tryna's mind, spilling over from Strand and Lynx's consciousness. In spite of the tragic history, she was excited see the world through her own eyes and to travel to the forbidden lands. She walked with an anxious energy she could only describe as preternatural. Was it the embodiment of both Lynx and Strand that gave her such electricity she wondered as she covered the miles easily? The Mamaroneck crossing was marked—as Nelson had described—by a pair of ragged shoes suspended by their laces from the no longer used power lines above. She released the animals to let them relieve themselves while she watched for a ferry.

Less than three hours later a skimpy flat boat motored up to a dock hidden by overgrowth. Strand quickly tucked her thick silver hair under her large green crocheted cap, stepped from the shadow of trees and turned to call for Sliver and Dot. Before she could speak they were there waiting, assessing the new arrival.

"Been here long?" The ferryer asked as he stepped onto shore.

"About two hours." "

Tryna watched him warily; Nelson had told her Society was capable of any trickery to recapture anyone they thought of as property.

The man appeared to be white and in his sixties; under his snug, watch cap his pale eyes were also cautious. His was an illegal service since travel away from Society City toward the Great Sunders was supposed to be carefully supervised as it had been when Lynx petitioned to visit her mother.

She said as little as possible hoping to hear spoken a word Nelson had told her to listen for when uncertain of her next step.

"Seen any other folks?"

"Just us."

"See any *wolverines* out here while you were waiting, did you?"

The two clamored inside and Tryna couldn't stop herself smiling.

"No, but I was hoping to."

The ferryer grinned too, and stretched out his hand.

"Archibald be my name today."

"I'm..."

"No need. You may have another name by tomorrow." He laughed contagiously as if he'd discovered the oldest joke on earth. Tryna laughed with him as she loaded the backpack onto the ferry and watched Dot and Sliver slip back into their carrier.

"Put this on," Archibald said handing Tryna a thick, brown rubber slicker that came down to her ankles. "It can get wet on a river." He laughed again, and then said, "Tell me a story."

Tryna was puzzled, "Story?"

"Yep, that's your fare to cross. Could be true, could be made up of whole cloth. I just like a story."

Tryna wasn't sure how to tell a story. She really had no past of her own. So, she sat, holding tightly to the flotation ring Archibald had given her in case of an accident. She let

Lynx speak.

"When I was a child all the others made fun of me especially as my hair started to turn white, marking me as an empath. I was awkward...shy; I didn't know what to say when they teased." Tryna listened to her voice; which was really Lynx.

"I was so afraid of them I couldn't see their fear. Where we lived my mother kept me close and I felt the most free when I went out to the pasture and sat with the cows. One in particular, our best milker, seemed to recognize me. Silly I know, but she let me brush her hide just like my mother brushed my hair. She was beautiful, brown and white with those huge bovine eyes and I loved her so much. She'd come to the fence when I started toward the pasture as if she wanted to see me.

"I realized that's really what most of us long for: someone to not turn away but just come to the fence like they want to see us. So, the next time the kids were passing our house they clickity-clacked their sticks across our fence and tossed their insults at me as usual, not expecting me to respond. But this time I walked to the fence and smiled. They were so confused I laughed."

"Did that teach them?"

"I'm not sure. The last one threw his stick and it bounced off my head. They laughed as they ran away. But I wasn't afraid of them anymore, so I wasn't much fun to torment."

"It's hard to imagine you being afraid."

"We're all afraid of something aren't we;" Tryna answered, "sometimes more than one something."

"Guess you're right about that. What're you afraid of now?"

"Not knowing enough. Seeing...our...mother."

"I think mothers stay the same through the years...if she was good before she's good now."

"But I've changed, more than I can explain to her."

"Probably don't matter, if she's as good as you remember."

Tryna didn't respond. Everything was new and odd to her so the Great Sunders simply made her curious. But she worried about Lynx's mother—a stranger who was meant to know her, love her and help her survive the journey. Tryna didn't know why the idea of 'mother' frightened her so. Lynx clearly had a strong relationship with this woman who'd reluctantly given her up to Society's officials. Strand, on the other hand, had been raised in an orphanage with only suspicion for her missing mother. Tryna had trouble untangling the strands of emotion so took a deep breath and focused on the river for a while.

"May I ask you a question?"

"Ask it."

"Do you ever ferry people back the other way; west to east back to Society?"

"Not too often. They don't usually have good stories to tell."

"Another?"

"Go ahead."

"Have you been out to the Great Sunders?"

"Yep." He was silent for a moment, gathering his thoughts to make a picture.

"They created untold death and destruction, you see, but they're mighty beautiful things. The land drops away and seems to disappear into nothing, at least where I was. Now there's roads, but..."

"Roads?"

"Sure, you think people going to go anywhere without roads? Some old highway, but mostly they follow the old paths the Native Peoples used a couple hundred years ago. The tribes seem to remember them easy enough. Not much motor traffic, you see, so they're not much. Fit into the forest and follow rivers. Beautiful, you see. Wild animals are kind of nerve-wracking. They told you about that right?"

Tryna searched her short memory and heard Nelson's voice warning her to listen to her animals' warnings about any approaching beasts.

"Yes." Then she asked: "Native Tribes?"

"Yep!" He said enthusiastically. "They spring back like flowers waiting for water. Some blended, some original, kind of exciting. There's all manner of villages, all manner of folks. And all the dreamers! You'll have a grand time, I bet."

That wasn't how Tryna would have described running for her life but better that than succumb to the terror that crept around the edges of her consciousness. He glanced at a strand of her silver hair escaping the cap and said, "You being followed, I presume...don't answer. Those animals you got will be on the alert, you pay attention to them.

He recognized the mark of an empath and didn't want

104

to probe more so was silent the remainder of the trip. Soon they were settling into the approach to the western dock. Archibald helped her with her pack and the animals onto a more stable dock than she'd left on the eastern shore.

"You're going to want to make your way south toward the old automobile tunnels. Within

three hours, less if you're as good a walker as you look, you'll come across the bikeways

depot at dusk. You can pick up whichever kind of transport you fancy--one wheel to eight. They

got good water and can show you what to look out for in terms of contamination this side of Ramapo Sunder. Things are all clear if you're going out past New Madrid Sunder but you got to pay attention afore that."

Tryna stuck out her hand automatically to shake Archibald's. He took a step back and gave a small smile.

"No thanks," Archibald said then hopped back onto the ferry and started the engine.

Of course, he'd be afraid to touch an empath Tryna remembered. The weight of the strangeness of the encounter and mystery of what lie ahead dropped onto her shoulders.

"Thank you for the ride."

"Thank you for the story. Go west!" He sang out his final greeting.

Tryna walked slowly taking in the ruined landscape around her. High rises were empty, some were caved in upon themselves where plant life reclaimed them. Few lights dotted the landscape as dusk slipped in around her. After several miles, a huge warehouse loomed ahead as if had been obscured by clouds that parted as she approached. All sides were decorated with wheels of varied colours and sizes.

Bikeways it is, Tryna thought and let Sliver and Dot out of the carrier. They sniffed the air and chased each other into high grass then returned just as Tryna set down their food tablets and water bowl.

"I'm not sure how this works but let's get going," She said as if they needed her words out loud. They were as tuned into her thoughts as Lynx had been to Strand's. She approached the warehouse carefully and heard the tinkering of workers hammering on metal.

"Hello?"

An older woman, maybe 70 years old, with caramel-colored skin came toward her dressed in coveralls, her hands marked with grease. She looked at Tryna and her animal companions closely before she said, "Buenos tardes, mi hermana, I think three wheels, si?

"Si," Tryna answered, not sure how much Spanish she actually knew. "Gracias," she added.

The woman turned and Tryna followed her deeper into the warehouse where dozens of rows of bicycles stood ready. She stopped at a larger, three-wheeler with baskets in the front and the back and waved her hands to Tryna.

"Some piece of something, shirt, cloth something, here," she pointed at the front basket, "and animals will ride with you like the wind, si! The pack on the back. This one even has a compass here on the handle bars... deluxe!" And she laughed as if she were handing over the keys to a limousine.

Tryna loved the look of it. The sturdy frame and fat tires seemed to be made for her. She looked at the woman to ask about payment.

"The cycle is yours; we have heard you are coming. Pump is affixed there for repairs. The next warehouse is 100 miles so have no fears. Leave the cycle when you arrive home..."

"Home?"

"You go to see tu madre, sí?"

"Uh...sí."

"So, you may leave it there and someone will return it to a warehouse or you keep it for every day. As you wish. Send support when you can."

Home. Tryna's stomach turned over at that word. How could she explain who they were? It was as if she were telling a mother that her daughter was dead; except she wasn't, she was inside. The dilemma buzzed in her head like a thundering cicada so Strand spoke, her voice harsh and dark.

Push the unknowable aside, woman and get on with it!

"You do ride, don't you?" the older woman asked as she watched Tryna frozen amidst her inner conflict with Strand.

"Oh, uh, yes." 'I think,' Tryna added to herself, grateful for the balance of three wheels.

"Good!"

"Thank you. Gracias."

"De nada."

Once she'd loaded the cycle with her belongings and

animals, Tryna turned it toward the wide door and climbed onto the seat. She gave one last wave to the brown woman who shouted, "Vente oeste!" as she waved back.

Tryna had to watch the path carefully as she cycled, everything was in such disrepair but sometimes she just stopped to look at the landscape. Nature had reclaimed many abandoned structures so opulent greenery rose her. She knew from the paper map that Nelson had given her that it wasn't far to the farm where Lynx's mother lived. It was part of one of the certified outposts that Society allowed to survive as a feeder community, from which it could harvest food, pluck workers or when they were lucky empaths like Lynx.

Tryna didn't think about Society much until she stopped to sleep for the night. She unfurled the carefully packed fabric that emerged from the cross bar of her cycle and pegged it into the ground creating a shelter big enough for her, Sliver and Dot. As she zipped in, she felt watched but wasn't sure if it were animal or human. She realized Lynx and Strand who'd been quiet were murmuring frantically.

I knew they wouldn't let me go!
We didn't come this far to panic now.
They've sent people to bring me back!
Calm now we'll get to safety.
What if they try to take me back!

Tryna became rigid with anxiety as their voices bounced around in the little tent. Nelson had warned her to use the animals' calming techniques if necessary. She touched the tiny dog Sliver, who butted her with his cool nose. Dot kneaded Tryna's side for a few minutes then settled against her lowering her anxiety.

"There is no me." Tryna whispered to quiet them. "There's us." She then spoke only in her mind...where the actual trouble was. "They may be tracking us. Nelson said not to try to hide. But it's us now. We'll figure this out."

Tryna's muscles relaxed as Lynx and Strand were soothed by her voice. This was such a puzzle: the ones inside were her and not her. Was there a 'her' without them? How did they all adjust to this new way? How did she learn to live as the three of them? Fear crystallized into a hard knot in her stomach. She had to elude those Society might send after Lynx and Strand and tame her own mind.

She didn't sleep much. Each snap of a twig or shadow movement of a leaf felt like a bounty agent or a wild cat about to pounce. As if she were talking to Archibald Tryna told herself the story of the tattoo to reassure herself that even if someone did leap out the bushes at her she had papers, and she in no way resembled the women then called Lynx or Strand. She dropped off just before dawn.

She opened her eyes as Dot walked heavily back and forth across her stomach and saw Sliver at her feet alert, staring at the side of the tent. Then the click of metal was so out of place Tryna knew immediately there was danger. Tryna talked to the animals as if she'd heard nothing.

"Here boy, do you need to get out? Here you go," she said after reaching into her pack then casually offering Sliver a damp sponge which Sliver nipped. She

109

unzipped the small opening to let Sliver and Dot emerge. She slipped out too and did a dramatic stretch for her audience. The animals rustled in the bushes.

"Please don't move." A harsh light glared at her making it impossible to see who had the tremulous voice behind it. "I won't hurt you; we're going back together and nobody gets hurt."

Tryna guessed the man was over six feet tall from the angle of his voice, but she couldn't tell anything else. He clearly had some type of weapon or he wouldn't keep saying, ironically, 'no one was going to get hurt.'

"Your name is Lynx and Society wants you back, not harmed. Put these on," he said and Tryna heard the sound that had awakened her—handcuffs clinked together as they fell at her feet.

"No, I have papers. I'm not who you're looking for."

"Yeah, they warned me you might be disguised. I take you back and get my money and you all can sort it out."

"I promise you..."

"You're in disguise but those animals aren't! They told me about them. Let's make this easy, put the cuffs on."

Tryna didn't have to think what to do next as she heard Strand's voice guttural inside her head.

My turn! Down!

Tryna ducked as Sliver leapt out and fastened his teeth firmly on the man's wrist. A gun shot and a short, sharp scream pierced the predawn dark. Dot wound herself around his ankles and he fell to his knees silently. The substance Sliver had licked from Tryna's sponge,

110

non-toxic to animals, was paralyzing to humans when it entered their bloodstream; which it easily did when Sliver bit into the gun hand of the hunter. Tryna raised her foot to kick him but caught herself; or rather she caught Strand whose impulses had taken over.

"No!" Tryna backed away as if to save herself as much as to spare the bounty agent.

Sliver came to Tryna's side and barked once reminding her to give him water so his mouth was clean again. She filled his water dish from her bottle then heard Dot pushing the handcuffs. Tryna nodded then slipped them onto the agent. As she watched his unconscious body, she realized he would be completely at the mercy of any animals that hunted in the woods. Most would be simply feral cats or dogs that were surviving as best they could but wolves or bears would not be so benign.

Forget that sickening lump!

We mustn't leave him!

He'd have dragged us back and let them hook us to a machine until we...

"Please let me think. I don't want to just leave him," Tryna pleaded while she tried to imagine what she could do to protect him until another traveler found him. She discovered it was impossibly easy to lift him. Clearly, she had not just the inner voices of three but the strength of three as well.

She assembled a rough platform from tree limbs and nestled it on some branches; precarious but at least above the ground. She threw the bounty agent's still inert body easily over her shoulder in a firefighter's carry and gripped

111

the trunk of the tree as if she were in a playground. When she laid him out on the platform, she made sure he was curled up so his feet didn't hang down low enough for a random wolf or fox or whatever roamed the woods to gnaw on it.

Sliver and Dot watched patiently as she dropped easily back to the ground. Trembling started at her feet and crawled up her body to her shoulders. The adrenaline was gone and it was quiet as if Strand and Lynx had gone back to sleep leaving her with the aftermath of terror. She jumped up and down a couple of times as if she could drop the ring of fear from around her down into the ground. It worked.

"Guess we're up now. Might as well get back on the road."

Tryna repacked the tent into her cycle; loaded Sliver and Dot into the basket which she'd discovered had a cleverly hidden hood to cut the wind. The morning sky was brightening but Tryna didn't want to take any chances with the untended roads so she pulled a head lamp from her bag to affix to the large helmet she fastened over her hat.

Two more days and nights but no other agents followed. She worried that Society would send them directly to the mother's farm but according to Nelson she dare not bypass it. On the third morning she pulled out her map and gauged her location. At the speed she was travelling she imagined she was not too far into New Jersey but she didn't see any landmarks to help her pin it down more precisely. Again, she felt the tug of anxiety.

She only knew of 'mothers' through Lynx's feelings and images. Would the mother know her? Or turn her into Society. She'd clearly let her daughter be taken; how much should she be trusted?

My mother is the soul of honest!

She has never seen this you, though

She will know me no matter what form.

She may know a little freckled red head but what does that look like next to a muscular dark woman? Be real, okay.

She'll see me and only me, Tryna thought. And I don't even know how I feel about me. Black? White? Other?"

We're a...

...a pentimento!

No, we're...an assemblage, the past and present together.

However you say it we're the best of all of us.

Right! A bit of this, that and the other.

Tryna found she couldn't take part in the debate since she had no real experience that preceded waking up and running. All her information was second hand. So, as she cycled, she listened to Lynx and Strand exploring their memories of Society's attempts to control the world around them and their ideas of who they were now. It was like having a play...a very talky play...unfolding in her head. All the while she scanned her surroundings in case another bounty hunter was lurking, ready to return her to the cage she'd escaped.

Tryna, Sliver and Dot travelled for the balance of the day, stopping once at the summit of a hill to eat and survey the landscape from the shade of a stand of evergreens. Tryna was just wondering what the ferryer had meant when he said that there were 'Dreamers' when she felt Lynx begin to vibrate inside.

There! There! Turn, we're almost there.

Tryna started to mount the cycle when she heard one of the voices shout:

Stop!

What is that?

That's not...

Tryna dug a scope out of the pack and peered down where she noted a barely hidden shelter; it was a bit in from the road as it turned toward the farm. She scanned the surroundings and located an unlikely pile of branches about a quarter of a mile past the hidden blind. She was certain the bounty hunter's conveyance was secreted there, waiting to take his prey back to Society City. Tryna took a deep breath and the voices were oddly quiet as if they'd finally accepted that she was in charge. But no one could be more uncertain than Tryna. Using the scope, she surveyed the area again. She lowered the animals from their perch on the cycle and again tinctured the tips of Sliver's teeth with the paralising agent.

They moved quietly down the hill toward the blind which Tryna hoped hid only one tracker. It occurred to her that perhaps they'd killed Lynx's mother.

NO! I feel her, she's there!

Tryna stopped to listen and realised she too could feel the mother was alive. She noted the sneakers hanging incongruously from a high tree branch as the animals trotted ahead and she relaxed a bit. She thought the blind was cloaked because she couldn't identify anyone inside. She circled around, deeper into the wood until she thought she was far enough behind the tracker's hiding spot. It was too late when she noticed the small circle scope that emerged from the top of the blind. Its camera was sure to have revealed her presence to the bounty agent where he was hiding.

Just as she understood this she was struck in her mid-back from behind. She rolled over quickly to see the bounty hunter. His lopsided face was like a nightmare mask that grinned down at her. His jaw was askew and his head looked as if had been caved in. A 'Frankenstein' she thought, remembering something Lynx had said. She shook her head and noted the dart gun pointed at her. Not a monster, she thought; he or his mother must have been damaged in the poisonous fallout from the ruptures. Sliver and Dot were bounding back through the brush but Tryna was sure they couldn't disarm him in time. She heard a whistle cut through the air and rolled but felt a dart slice her side. She looked up in time to see the bounty hunter also crumple to the ground.

A swooping yelp filled the air as one woman broke through the brush behind the animals and another dropped from the trees beneath which Tryna had just passed. They wore a mix of earth toned pants, shirts and scarves; leather gloves protected their hands as they swung their bows across their shoulders. The thin one was taller than Tryna, and as dark as the bark of the tree from which she'd descended. She rushed to Tryna and ordered:

"Still," as she investigated the wound. The other was blonde and plump with a smile as wide as the valley below.

"Not bad," the tall one said, pulled a pad from her shoulder pack, lifted Tryna's shirt and pressed it until the pad absorbed the blood and adhered.

"Did you see any wolverine on the journey?"

"No, but I was hoping to," Tryna responded relieved to hear the word confirming safety.

"Let's go back for your cycle," she said, turning back up the hill. "You got this?" she asked the other.

"Done," came the terse replay that barely interrupted her smile. "Y'all don't tarry here long with your mama. Me and her will pick you up on the other side, 24 hours," she drawled then winked at Tryna as the taller woman reached down and swung the eerily still hunter up to her shoulder.

"Where...?" Tryna started to ask.

The freckled woman pressed her finger to her lips signaling silence. Tryna touched the place where the dart had cut into her side but felt little pain. She stood with Sliver and Dot then pulled her water bottle from her belt and bent down to rinse the tincture from Sliver's teeth. She stood to say thank you to the woman who'd helped rescue her but she was gone. Tryna hurried behind the tall woman to regain their cycle.

She trembled when she reached the cycle, realising how close they'd been to capture. The sight of the clunky, sturdy conveyance elicited such joy from Tryna she was startled.

"We'll collect you. Twenty-four hours. On the nose,

got it?"

Tryna nodded as the tall woman veered off into the woods her burden light on her shoulders.

Partisans

Dreamers

She loaded Sliver and Dot back onto the cycle, then glided down the hill toward the path that led off toward the farm. Within an hour they reached a fence; one Lynx remembered well.

We're here.

Calm down. It'll be okay.

Tryna wasn't sure if Strand had meant that for her or Lynx but it didn't sooth her one bit. She lifted the gate and walked toward the small house set far back from the road. She heard the scratching of animals, chickens she realized, and a low sound. As she walked on the path uncertainty rippled through her body like a laser disassembling all of her courage. On her left cows fed in a small pasture. One lumbered toward the fence close to the house, it's huge brown and white head threaded with silver.

As Tryna came abreast of her the cow thrust her head over the fence almost butting her. Strand pulled back inside, protective; but Lynx's impulse made Tryna reach out and caress the milker's head. A wave of calm washed over Tryna as she gazed into the large round eyes that stared back as if she knew her.

Recognition flowed through them all like an electric current. Tryna understood now why she'd been directed to make this stop even though it was certain to be the prime place bounty hunters would search. The animal who'd been Lynx's refuge raised its sliver flecked head pressing into Tryna's hand more firmly. She made that deep bovine sound then looked again into Tryna's eyes. Then she felt it; the gaze forged a bond that annealed the three women together. Their voices blended into a gentle hum beneath Tryna's thoughts; they would remain a chorus inside her, lending their voices and their strengths. The milker eased back away from the fence. With this link Nelson's magic was complete. Whatever happened in her travels forward, whatever challenges and adventures Tryna would think, feel and act as three. It was a gift that could save her or drive her mad.

Tryna watched the milker lumber back toward her herd; anxiously Tryna turned to the farm house, still a quarter mile down the road. Without using the scope, Tryna could see a mother smiling at her from the doorway.

END

Jewelle Gomez, (Cabo Verdean/Wampanoag/Ioway; she/her), is a novelist, poet, essayist, playwright, and lesbian/feminist activist. Her eleven books include five collections of poetry and the first Black Lesbian vampire novel, *THE GILDA STORIES*. In print for more than 30 years, the novel was recently optioned by Cheryl Dunye ("Lovecraft Country" "Watermelon Woman") for a TV mini-series. Her latest collection of poetry, "Still Water," is from BLF Press.

Her work has appeared in numerous anthologies including: *Red Indian Road West*, *Dark Matter: A Century of Speculative Fiction from the African Diaspora*, *Oxford Treasury of Love Stories*, *Luminescent Threads: Connections to Octavia Butler*, and *Stories for Chip: A Tribute to Samuel R. Delany*.

Gomez was playwright in residence (2011-2023) at New Conservatory Theatre Center (San Francisco) which commissioned and produced her last three plays: "Waiting for Giovanni" about author/activist James Baldwin; "Leaving the Blues" about singer/composer Alberta Hunter, and "Unpacking in P'town" about a group of retired vaudevillians.

She was the recipient of an NEA Fellowship, two California Arts Council Artist's Residency and recently a Bram Stoker Legacy Award from the Horror Writers of America.

Connect with her on Instagram: @VampyreVamp. www.jewellegomez.com